CAMI KOEPP

Fading Into Mist

This book was professionally typeset on Reedsy.
Find out more at reedsy.com

Contents

One

A Chance Encounter

The forest seemed alive that morning, cloaked in a soft mist that blurred the edges of reality. Each step Lena Cross took felt like walking into a dream. Her sketchbook was clutched tightly in one hand, the other brushing against damp foliage as she moved deeper into the woods. The earth beneath her feet was damp and spongy, muffling her footsteps, and the air carried a weighty stillness that felt almost sacred.

Lena was no stranger to solitude, but this forest—its towering pines and gnarled oaks—held an eerie silence that unsettled even her. She adjusted her scarf against the crisp air, muttering to herself as if her voice could anchor her. Just a quick sketch… I'll be out of here in no time.

She had heard rumors about this place—the Mistwood Forest, a name locals whispered with a mix of reverence and fear. It was said to be enchanted, cursed, or both. But Lena, ever the skeptic, dismissed the stories as local folklore. She wasn't here for ghost stories. She was here for inspiration, to capture the otherworldly beauty she couldn't find in the bustling city.

Her breath caught when she stumbled into a clearing. Before her stood a cabin—ancient and weathered, its wood darkened by years of rain and time. Moss clung to its walls, and the windows, though broken, glimmered faintly in the gray light. It was like something out of her grandmother's bedtime stories, both inviting and forbidding.

Compelled by an inexplicable pull, Lena stepped closer, flipping open her sketchbook. Her pencil scratched against the paper as she worked quickly, her gaze darting between the cabin and her page. Her heart raced, though she couldn't say why. It wasn't fear exactly. It was something deeper, something she couldn't name.

The sound of a camera shutter snapped her out of her trance.

She turned sharply, nearly dropping her sketchbook. A man stood at the edge of the clearing, half-hidden by the mist. He was tall, with dark hair that fell in messy waves around his face. A camera hung around his neck, its lens pointed directly at her. His presence was as jarring as a thunderclap in the silence.

Who are you? she demanded, her voice harsher than she intended. She stepped back, clutching her pencil like a weapon.

The man lowered the camera, his lips curling into a small, apologetic smile. Sorry. I didn't mean to startle you. His voice was deep, smooth, with a faint edge of something she couldn't place.

You didn't answer my question, she said, narrowing her eyes.

I'm Ethan. He gestured toward the camera. I'm a photographer. I was… capturing the mist.

Lena raised an eyebrow. Capturing me, more like.

His smile widened, though his eyes remained serious. You were part of the scene. I didn't mean any harm.

There was something about him—an intensity in his gaze, as if he were trying to unravel her with a single look. It made her uneasy, yet she couldn't bring herself to walk away.

I don't like being photographed without permission, she said, her tone colder than she felt.

Ethan nodded, slipping the camera strap over his shoulder. Fair enough. I'll delete the shot.

Before she could respond, he approached her, his steps careful, deliberate. He moved as if he belonged in the forest, his presence somehow amplifying the surreal atmosphere. When he stopped a few feet away, he held out a hand. Let me make it up to you. I'll show you the best view of the forest—no cameras involved.

Lena hesitated. Everything about him felt like a contradiction. He was both disarming and unsettling, a stranger who seemed to know exactly how to lure her in. But curiosity outweighed caution. Against her better judgment, she nodded.

Ethan led her deeper into the woods, their steps crunching softly against the underbrush. He didn't speak much, and when he did, his words carried a cryptic weight. He told her about the light at certain times of the day, how it transformed the forest into something otherworldly. She found herself drawn to his voice, to the way he spoke as if the forest were a living thing with secrets to share.

They stopped at a small hill overlooking a valley shrouded in mist. The sun, weak and pale, broke through the clouds just enough to illuminate the landscape. It was breathtaking—like stepping into a painting.

Lena was about to thank him when she noticed something strange. In the distance, near the edge of the valley, a faint figure moved. It was barely more than a silhouette, but it was unmistakable—a person, walking through the mist.

Who's that? she asked, pointing.

Ethan stiffened. For the first time, his composure faltered. His eyes narrowed, and his jaw tightened as he stared at the figure.

No one, he said sharply. Too sharply.

That's not 'no one,' Lena argued. Do you know them?

Ethan didn't answer. Instead, he turned to her, his expression a mix of fear and urgency. We need to go. Now.

The air seemed to grow colder, heavier, as if the forest itself were closing in on them. Lena's heart raced as Ethan grabbed her wrist, pulling her away from the hill.

What's going on? she demanded, struggling to keep up with his long strides.

I'll explain later, he said, his voice tight. Just trust me.

But Lena didn't trust him—not fully. She glanced over her shoulder as they hurried through the trees, and her stomach dropped. The figure in the mist was closer now, moving faster than seemed possible.

Ethan, she whispered, her voice trembling. It's following us.

He didn't reply. His grip on her wrist tightened, and his pace quickened. The forest blurred around them, the mist thickening until Lena could barely see the path ahead.

When they finally reached the edge of the woods, Ethan stopped abruptly, turning to face her. His expression was unreadable, but his eyes burned with an intensity that sent a shiver down her spine.

You need to stay away from the cabin, he said, his voice low, almost a growl. Promise me, Lena. Don't go back there.

Before she could respond, he stepped back into the forest and disappeared into the mist, leaving her alone with nothing but the echo of his warning and the chilling memory of the figure that had followed them.

Two

Shadows in the Frame

The gallery was alive with a low hum of voices, punctuated by the occasional clink of champagne glasses. Lena stepped through the grand entrance, the pale light from crystal chandeliers illuminating the sparse crowd of art enthusiasts. It was Ethan's photography exhibition, his invitation still tucked inside her bag like a puzzle piece she hadn't yet decided how to fit into her life.

Draped in a simple black dress, Lena felt out of place among the tailored suits and high heels. Her nerves hummed beneath her skin as her gaze swept the room. The photographs, large and unframed, hung in deliberate disarray, each piece drawing visitors into a world shrouded in shadow and light. Mist, forests, and fleeting figures were recurring themes.

She caught sight of Ethan near the center of the room. He stood in front of a group of admirers, his dark hair slightly disheveled, his black suit fitting him like a second skin. His posture was casual, but his sharp, restless gaze betrayed an underlying tension. When their eyes met, a flicker of something unspoken passed between them.

Ethan excused himself from his circle of admirers, making his way toward her with purposeful strides. As he approached, Lena felt the pull of his presence, an inexplicable magnetism that both intrigued and unnerved her.

I'm glad you came, he said, his voice smooth but tinged with something she couldn't name. Relief? Anxiety?

I wasn't sure if I would, she admitted, crossing her arms. But I'm curious about your work.

Ethan smiled, a shadow of mischief dancing in his eyes. Curiosity can be dangerous.

So I've heard, she replied, her tone dry but her lips betraying a small smile. Show me something worth the risk.

He gestured for her to follow him, weaving through the clusters of guests. As they walked, Lena felt the weight of his attention, as though he were studying her reactions, cataloging them for later. They stopped in front of a series of black-and-white photographs arranged in a jagged line across the wall.

These are from Mistwood, Ethan said quietly.

Lena's breath caught as she took in the images. Each frame was hauntingly beautiful—a kaleidoscope of shifting light and shadow. The forest seemed alive, its mist curling like tendrils around gnarled trees and forgotten paths. But it wasn't just the beauty of the landscapes that unsettled her. It was the shadows.

In nearly every photograph, there was a figure or a shape—sometimes faint, other times almost fully formed. A man standing at the edge of the trees, a woman half-hidden by mist, a shadow stretching across the ground where no one should have been. The figures were blurry, indistinct, and yet they seemed to pulse with an otherworldly presence.

They're beautiful, Lena said, her voice barely above a whisper. But… who are the people in them?

Ethan's expression darkened, and he glanced around the room before leaning closer. No one. At least, no one I saw when I took the photos.

Lena's skin prickled. What do you mean? These figures—they're in your shots. How could you not see them?

I don't know, Ethan said, his voice low. They weren't there when I was taking the pictures. But every time I developed them… they appeared.

Lena turned back to the photographs, her unease deepening. The shadows seemed to shift under her scrutiny, as though they were alive. Her eyes lingered on one image in particular—a shot of the cabin she had sketched just days ago. The photograph captured the building in stunning detail, its weathered wood and broken windows stark against the misty backdrop. But standing in the doorway was a figure—a woman, her face obscured, her body barely more than a silhouette.

That's the cabin, Lena said, her throat dry.

Ethan nodded. I thought it was just a trick of the light. But the more I looked at it, the more certain I became that she was… real. Or at least, she was there.

Lena's pulse quickened. Do you think it's Elise? The woman from the journal?

Ethan hesitated. I don't know. But there's something about that place—about her—that feels connected to me. To us.

Before Lena could respond, a voice interrupted them. Marvelous work, Mr.

Gray.

They turned to see an older man approaching, his silver hair slicked back, his suit tailored to perfection. His sharp blue eyes lingered on Ethan with a mix of admiration and something more calculating.

Victor, Ethan said curtly, his entire demeanor shifting. The easy charm he had shown with Lena vanished, replaced by a cold wariness.

Your photographs never cease to amaze, Victor said smoothly, ignoring Ethan's tension. He turned to Lena, his smile widening. And who is this lovely guest?

Lena, she said, her voice steady despite the discomfort creeping up her spine.

A pleasure, Lena. Victor's gaze lingered on her for a moment too long before returning to Ethan. I couldn't help but notice that your work grows darker with each exhibition. The shadows—so evocative. Almost as though they're trying to tell a story.

Ethan's jaw tightened. If you'll excuse us, Victor, we were just—

Leaving? Victor finished, his smile turning predatory. Of course. But do be careful, Ethan. Some stories are best left untold.

With that, Victor turned and disappeared into the crowd, leaving a palpable chill in his wake. Lena looked at Ethan, whose hands were clenched into fists.

Who was that? she asked.

Someone I should've seen coming, Ethan muttered. He glanced at the photographs again, his expression haunted. We need to talk. Not here.

Before Lena could protest, Ethan took her hand, pulling her toward the exit. The cool night air hit her like a slap as they stepped outside, but it did little to clear the questions swirling in her mind.

What's going on? she demanded. Who is Victor, and why does he seem to know so much about your work?

Ethan looked at her, his dark eyes filled with something she hadn't seen before: fear.

Victor isn't just anyone. He's tied to the shadows in the photographs. And if he's here… it means we're running out of time.

Lena froze, her heart pounding. Running out of time for what?

Ethan didn't answer. Instead, he turned his gaze toward the forest in the distance, its outline barely visible under the moonlight. For everything, he whispered.

The silence that followed was deafening, filled with questions Lena wasn't sure she wanted the answers to. But one thing was certain: she was already too deep to walk away.

Three

Whispers of the Cabin

The moon hung low in the sky, casting an eerie silver glow over Mistwood Forest. Lena stood at the edge of the clearing, her breath visible in the crisp night air. The cabin loomed ahead like a shadowy sentinel, its warped walls and broken windows shrouded in mist. She clutched her sketchbook against her chest, her pulse quickening as a familiar pull drew her closer.

Ethan's warning echoed in her mind. Stay away from the cabin.

But something deep inside her refused to listen. There were questions burning in her chest, secrets lurking in the folds of her memory that wouldn't leave her in peace. The cabin was the key. She knew it as surely as she knew her own name.

As she approached, the forest seemed to hold its breath. The crunch of leaves beneath her boots felt deafening in the silence, and the mist thickened, coiling around her ankles like living tendrils. The cabin's door creaked on its hinges, swaying gently as though inviting her in.

Lena hesitated. Her fingers brushed against the rough wood, the texture sending a shiver through her. The air here was colder, heavier, as though the cabin itself exhaled a deep and ancient sadness. Gathering her courage, she pushed the door open.

The inside was just as she remembered it from her first visit—dark, musty, and riddled with decay. Moonlight streamed through the broken windows, illuminating the scattered debris on the floor. Her eyes were drawn to the corner of the room, where an old wooden easel stood. A faded canvas sat upon it, the paint cracked and peeling.

Curiosity piqued, Lena moved closer. The painting depicted the forest, but it wasn't quite right. The trees were twisted, their branches clawing at a crimson sky. A figure stood in the distance, barely visible through the chaos of the strokes. It was a woman, her face obscured, her arms outstretched as if beckoning—or warning.

Lena's fingers traced the edge of the canvas, and a sudden chill coursed through her. She felt the unmistakable sensation of being watched. Whipping around, she scanned the room, her eyes darting to every shadow. The cabin was empty. But the feeling didn't fade.

She took a step back, her foot brushing against something solid. Looking down, she saw a small leather-bound book lying amidst the debris. Its cover was worn, the edges frayed, but the initials E.G. were still legible, embossed in faded gold. Her heart thudded in her chest as she picked it up, the leather cool against her skin.

The journal was brittle, the pages yellowed with age. Flipping through it, Lena found a series of sketches and notes, each more unsettling than the last. The drawings mirrored Ethan's photographs—shadowy figures lurking in the mist, their forms indistinct yet strangely human. Scrawled beneath one of the sketches were the words: She fades, and yet she remains.

What the hell… Lena whispered, her voice barely audible over the pounding of her heart.

The final pages of the journal were blank, save for a single entry scrawled in hurried, messy handwriting:

She called me back here tonight. The mist whispers her name. Elise. If I follow, I may never return, but I must try. I must find her. If anyone finds this journal, leave this place. It will not let you go.

Lena's fingers trembled as she clutched the journal to her chest. The room seemed to grow colder, the shadows lengthening. The sound of footsteps echoed faintly from somewhere outside. She froze, her breath catching in her throat. Someone—or something—was out there.

The door creaked, swinging wider, as though pushed by an unseen hand. A dark silhouette appeared in the doorway, tall and imposing. For a moment, Lena's fear paralyzed her, her mind racing with every horror story she'd ever heard.

Lena.

The voice was low, familiar, and tinged with something she couldn't quite place—relief, or perhaps desperation. Ethan stepped into the room, his features illuminated by the pale moonlight. His dark eyes locked onto hers, narrowing as they fell on the journal in her hands.

You shouldn't be here, he said, his tone a mixture of anger and worry. I told you to stay away.

I couldn't, Lena shot back, her voice shaking. There's something here, Ethan. Something tied to us. Look at this. She held up the journal, her hands trembling. It has your initials.

Ethan's jaw tightened. He strode forward, snatching the journal from her hands. As he flipped through the pages, his expression darkened. Where did you find this?

On the floor, Lena said, her voice barely above a whisper. Ethan, what's going on? Who is Elise?

He didn't answer. Instead, he closed the journal with a snap and turned to the door. We need to leave. Now.

No, Lena said, planting her feet. Not until you tell me what's happening. Why are you so afraid of this place? Of her?

Ethan's hands clenched at his sides. Because she's not just a memory. She's still here. And if you stay any longer, she'll find you.

The words sent a shiver down Lena's spine, but she stood her ground. I'm not leaving without answers.

Before Ethan could respond, a low, haunting sound filled the air—a whisper, soft yet piercing, as though carried by the wind. The mist outside the cabin thickened, pressing against the windows like a living thing. Lena's breath hitched as she turned toward the sound, her pulse racing.

The whisper grew louder, more distinct. It wasn't just wind. It was a voice. A woman's voice. And it was calling her name.

Lena…

Her blood turned to ice. She looked to Ethan, but his expression only deepened her fear. His face was pale, his eyes wide with dread.

She knows you're here, he said, his voice barely audible. We have to go. Now.

Before either of them could move, the cabin door slammed shut with a deafening crash, the sound reverberating through the room. The shadows on the walls seemed to ripple and twist, reaching for them as the whisper turned into a chilling laugh.

The last thing Lena saw before the room plunged into darkness was Ethan's terrified face and the shadows closing in around them.

Four

Ethan's Confession

The darkness was absolute. Lena's breaths came shallow and quick, each exhale swallowed by the oppressive silence that had followed the slamming of the door. Her hands instinctively reached out, searching for anything solid, anything real, and found Ethan's arm. His muscles were tense under her grip, like a coiled spring ready to snap.

Ethan, she whispered, her voice trembling. What's happening?

Stay close, he murmured. His voice was tight, controlled, but Lena could hear the undertone of fear. Whatever you do, don't let go of me.

The cabin groaned as though it were alive, the wooden beams creaking under some unseen weight. The shadows on the walls writhed, their movements unnatural, chaotic. Lena's pulse pounded in her ears, drowning out all rational thought.

The voice returned, low and melodic, a ghostly echo that seeped into her bones.

Lena…

It wasn't just a whisper now. It was a plea, a beckoning that sent chills racing down her spine. She clenched her jaw, fighting the urge to respond, to call out to the voice that seemed to know her name.

Ethan's grip on her arm tightened. Don't listen to it. Don't speak.

The shadows thickened, stretching toward them like skeletal hands. The air grew colder, each breath clouding in front of Lena's face. Her fingers dug into Ethan's sleeve, desperate for something to anchor her to reality.

Why is it calling me? she finally managed to choke out, her voice barely audible over the sinister whispers that filled the room.

It's not her, Ethan said, his tone clipped. Not really.

Who? Lena demanded, panic threading through her words. Who isn't it?

Elise, he said, his voice cracking on the name. She's gone. What's left… isn't her.

Lena's heart sank. The weight of his words pressed against her, heavy with sorrow and regret. Before she could question him further, the floor beneath them shuddered violently. The cabin tilted, as if the earth itself were shifting.

Run! Ethan shouted, yanking her toward the door.

But the door wouldn't budge. The shadows surged, slamming against the wood with a force that shook the entire structure. Lena stumbled, clutching Ethan's arm to keep from falling.

Through the chaos, she caught a glimpse of something in the shadows—a face, pale and hollow-eyed, its mouth twisted in a grotesque smile. It was gone in an instant, but the image seared itself into her mind.

We can't stay here! she cried, panic clawing at her throat. Ethan, what do we do?

He didn't answer. Instead, he pulled her toward a shattered window. The jagged edges of glass glittered like teeth in the faint moonlight.

This way, he said, his voice urgent. Go, now!

Lena hesitated, fear rooting her to the spot. But the shadows were closing in, their inky forms seeping across the floor like spilled ink. Swallowing her terror, she climbed through the window, the sharp edges of the frame biting into her palms. Ethan followed, his movements quick and deliberate.

The moment they were outside, the air felt different—lighter, less suffocating. But the mist still clung to them, and the whispers persisted, more insistent now.

Lena… come back…

The voice was closer, almost at her ear. She turned instinctively, her eyes darting to the cabin. For a split second, she thought she saw someone standing in the doorway—a woman with long, dark hair, her face obscured by the mist. But when Lena blinked, the figure was gone.

Keep moving, Ethan urged, pulling her away.

They ran through the forest, their footsteps muffled by the thick carpet of moss and leaves. The mist swirled around them, twisting into shapes that seemed almost human. The whispers followed, growing louder, more desperate.

Ethan, Lena gasped, struggling to keep up. What aren't you telling me? What is this?

He didn't slow down, didn't look back. It's too dangerous to explain here.

Then when? she demanded, her voice breaking. When are you going to stop running and tell me the truth?

Ethan stopped abruptly, turning to face her. His dark eyes burned with an intensity that made her heart skip a beat. When we're somewhere safe, he said firmly. And not a second before.

Before Lena could argue, the ground beneath her feet shifted. She stumbled, falling to her knees. Ethan knelt beside her, his hand on her shoulder.

Are you okay? he asked, his voice softer now.

Lena nodded, though her hands trembled as she brushed dirt from her palms. I saw her, she whispered. In the cabin. Or… something like her.

Ethan's jaw tightened. It's not her, he repeated, as though saying it aloud would make it true. Elise is gone. Whatever that thing is, it's not her.

Then who is she? Lena asked, her voice breaking. And why does she want me?

For a long moment, Ethan didn't answer. When he finally spoke, his voice was heavy with regret. She's a fragment. A memory that refuses to fade. She's tied to this forest, to me… and now, to you.

Lena stared at him, the weight of his words sinking in. What did you do, Ethan?

The question hung in the air, sharp and accusing. Ethan's gaze dropped, his shoulders slumping under an invisible burden.

I loved her, he said, his voice barely audible. And because of that, I lost her. I lost everything.

Before Lena could process his confession, the forest erupted with noise. The whispers turned into a deafening roar, the mist swirling violently around them. Shadows emerged from the trees, their forms more distinct now—humanoid, but wrong. Their limbs were too long, their movements jerky and unnatural.

Ethan grabbed Lena's hand, pulling her to her feet. Run, he said, his voice raw with desperation. Run and don't look back.

But as they fled deeper into the forest, the shadows followed, their distorted figures closing in. The voice—Elise's voice—rose above the chaos, filled with anguish.

Ethan… you can't escape me…

And then, just as the shadows seemed ready to engulf them, Lena tripped over something solid. She hit the ground hard, the breath knocked from her lungs. When she looked up, she saw a dark, ancient tree, its bark carved with symbols she didn't recognize.

Ethan froze, his eyes wide with horror. No, he whispered. Not here.

The tree seemed to pulse with energy, the symbols glowing faintly. The mist thickened, the air vibrating with a low hum. Lena's heart raced as she realized they hadn't escaped the danger—they'd run straight into the heart of it.

The whispers surrounded them, a single, chilling word echoing through the forest:

Stay.

Five

The Journal

The cabin's silence was suffocating, broken only by the faint creak of its weathered wooden boards beneath Lena's feet. The late afternoon sun filtered through the broken windowpanes, casting long, fractured shadows across the room. Dust floated in the air, shimmering like tiny fragments of another time.

Lena's fingers trembled as they hovered over the small leather-bound book she had found tucked beneath the loose floorboard. Its cover was worn, the edges frayed as though it had been handled countless times. A faint metallic scent lingered on it, the scent of age and secrets long hidden.

She glanced back toward the door, half-expecting Ethan to appear. He had gone to explore the nearby clearing, leaving her alone with her thoughts—and the eerie pull of this abandoned cabin. She swallowed hard and opened the journal.

The first page greeted her with a flowing script that sent a shiver down her spine. It was elegant yet urgent, the kind of handwriting that belonged to someone who wrote as if their life depended on it.

June 4th, 1973

She is everything I never dared dream of. Her laughter dances on the wind, her touch ignites the very air around her. And yet, the mist watches. It waits. I fear what it will take from us.

Lena's brow furrowed. The words felt intimate, raw, as though they weren't meant to be read by anyone else. She flipped the page, her curiosity overpowering the unease curling in her stomach.

June 18th, 1973

Elise says the mist is harmless, a mere trick of the forest's breath. But I know better. It moves with intent. It whispers when she isn't listening. I see the way it curls around her when she laughs, as though it knows she doesn't belong here. I cannot lose her. I won't.

The name Elise struck her like a thunderclap. The same name the towns-people had murmured with reverence and sorrow. Her hands shook as she flipped to the next entry, the words growing more frantic with each page.

July 1st, 1973

I begged her not to go to the cabin alone, but Elise is headstrong. Brave. Beautiful. The mist grows stronger every day, and I fear it has marked her. I don't know what it wants, but it will not have her. It cannot.

Lena's breath quickened. The voice behind the words seemed to leap off the page, desperate and raw. She glanced at the signature at the bottom of the last entry and froze.

E.G.

Her mind raced. Ethan had mentioned his family once owning this cabin, but he'd never elaborated. Could this journal belong to one of them? She flipped through the remaining pages, her eyes scanning for more answers, but the entries became more fragmented, more frenzied.

July 10th, 1973

The mist is alive. It took her. I saw it. One moment, she was there, her hand in mine, and the next... she was gone. Swallowed by the mist. I screamed her name until my throat was raw, but she didn't answer. She never answered.

The words trailed off into jagged scratches, the ink smeared as though the writer's hand had trembled uncontrollably. Lena's heart pounded in her chest. She flipped to the final page, her hands trembling.

July 13th, 1973

She disappeared into the mist.

The journal fell from Lena's hands, hitting the floor with a soft thud. The words echoed in her mind, heavy and suffocating. She turned toward the window, her gaze drawn to the forest beyond. The mist hung low over the trees, coiling lazily like a predator biding its time.

Lena?

She spun around, clutching her chest. Ethan stood in the doorway, his expression a mixture of concern and curiosity. He stepped inside, his boots creaking against the wooden floor. What's wrong?

I found this, she said, her voice unsteady as she gestured to the journal on the floor. You need to see it.

Ethan frowned but crossed the room, crouching to pick up the journal. He flipped through the pages, his brow furrowing deeper with each entry he read. When he reached the final page, his hands tightened around the leather cover, his knuckles turning white.

E.G., he murmured, his voice barely audible.

Do you know who that is? Lena asked, though she suspected the answer.

Ethan hesitated, his eyes distant. Ethan Gray. My great-uncle. This was his cabin.

Lena's stomach twisted. Then the woman… Elise?

Ethan nodded, his expression dark. She was his fiancée. The family always said she vanished in the forest, but no one knew how. Now we do.

A heavy silence filled the room, broken only by the faint rustle of leaves outside. Lena's gaze drifted to the journal in Ethan's hands, her thoughts racing.

This isn't just a story, she said quietly. It's a warning.

Ethan looked at her, his dark eyes unreadable. A warning for what?

For us, Lena said, her voice barely above a whisper. The mist isn't gone, Ethan. It's still here.

As if in response, a faint tendril of mist curled through the broken window, slithering into the room like a silent predator. It hovered between them for a moment, its presence sending a chill down Lena's spine, before retreating back into the forest.

Ethan closed the journal with a snap, his expression hardening. Then we'll find out what it wants, he said, his voice resolute. And we'll end this.

Lena nodded, though fear clawed at her chest. She knew this was only the beginning.

Six

An Unexpected Proposal

The cabin felt colder now, as if the tendril of mist had stolen something vital from the air before slipping away. Lena stood by the window, staring out at the forest. The trees seemed taller, darker, their silhouettes sharp against the fading light of the evening. She wrapped her arms around herself, the journal's haunting words still echoing in her mind.

Behind her, Ethan paced the length of the room, the journal clutched tightly in his hands. His movements were sharp, restless, and his expression was distant, as though he were lost in the past the journal had unearthed.

We can't ignore this, Lena said, breaking the silence.

Ethan stopped mid-step and turned to face her. I'm not ignoring it, he said, his voice quiet but firm. But we need more than this journal. We need answers.

And how do you suggest we get them? Lena asked, her voice tinged with frustration. Do you want to go back into the forest and ask the mist what it wants?

Ethan didn't respond immediately. He placed the journal on the small, dust-covered table in the center of the room, his fingers lingering on its worn cover. Not exactly, he said finally, his tone measured. But I think the journal is only part of the story. There's more out there—more we need to find.

Lena frowned. More? Like what?

Evidence, Ethan said, his gaze intense. Clues, pieces of the past that might help us understand what happened to Elise. If we can figure out why the mist took her, maybe we can figure out how to stop it.

Lena shook her head, her stomach twisting at the thought of venturing deeper into the forest. Ethan, we barely made it out of there last time. You saw what it's capable of. Do you really want to risk going back?

It's not about what I want, Ethan said, his voice rising. This isn't just about Elise anymore, Lena. It's about us.

The words hung in the air, heavy and unspoken. Lena's chest tightened, her thoughts racing. The journal's entries had felt personal, hauntingly so. The way Ethan had looked at her when he said us only deepened her unease.

What do you mean? she asked, her voice barely above a whisper.

Ethan hesitated, his hands clenching at his sides. I mean... there's a connection here, he said, his tone softer now. Between you, me, and all of this. The journal, the mist, the cabin—it's not random. It's like we were meant to find it.

Lena's pulse quickened. She wanted to dismiss his words as coincidence, but the unease in her chest wouldn't let her. She had felt it too—the inexplicable pull toward the cabin, the way the journal's words had resonated with her.

What are you saying? she asked cautiously.

Ethan took a step closer, his dark eyes searching hers. I'm saying we can't walk away from this, he said. I'm saying we need to see it through. Together.

Lena swallowed hard, her mind racing. Every instinct told her to walk away, to leave the cabin and the forest behind before it consumed them. But another part of her—a smaller, quieter voice—urged her to stay. To face the darkness and the mysteries it held.

And how do we do that? she asked, her voice trembling.

Ethan's expression softened, and he reached out to take her hands in his. His touch was warm, steady, grounding. Come with me, he said. On a journey. We'll retrace the story in the journal, follow the clues, and uncover the truth about Elise. We'll find out what the mist wants and why it's still here.

Lena stared at him, her heart pounding. You want to go looking for something that's clearly dangerous? Ethan, this isn't a story. This is real.

I know it's real, Ethan said, his voice firm. But it's also real that the mist isn't going to leave us alone. If we don't face it, it'll keep coming.

Lena pulled her hands away, pacing to the other side of the room. Her thoughts spiraled, torn between fear and the undeniable pull of Ethan's proposal. And what if we don't find anything? she asked, turning to face him. What if this all ends with us disappearing into the mist too?

Ethan's jaw tightened. Then at least we'll have tried. At least we won't have let it win.

The room fell silent, the weight of his words pressing down on Lena's chest. She looked out the window again, her gaze drifting to the forest. The mist lingered at the edges of the trees, curling like smoke, as if it were watching. Waiting.

She took a deep breath, her hands trembling at her sides. Okay, she said finally, her voice barely audible. I'll go.

Ethan's expression softened, relief flickering in his dark eyes. Thank you.

But, Lena added quickly, holding up a hand, we do this carefully. No wandering off alone, no taking unnecessary risks. If it gets too dangerous, we leave.

Agreed, Ethan said, his voice steady.

Lena nodded, though the unease in her chest didn't fade. She turned back to the journal, its worn cover seeming to stare back at her. The journey ahead felt impossibly daunting, the shadows of the past and the present converging into something far greater than either of them could understand.

But she knew there was no turning back now.

Seven

Echoes of the Past

The morning sun barely penetrated the thick canopy of trees, its weak rays filtering through the dense foliage in fractured beams. The forest felt different now, quieter and heavier, as if the air itself held secrets waiting to be revealed. Lena tightened her grip on the leather strap of her bag, her eyes scanning the path ahead. Beside her, Ethan walked with determined strides, the journal tucked securely under his arm.

They had followed the map sketched in the journal, leading them to a nearby village at the forest's edge. The journal had mentioned it briefly—a place Elise and Ethan's great-uncle had visited frequently. Lena couldn't shake the feeling that they were walking into something much larger than themselves.

As they approached the first few scattered houses, Lena noticed the way the villagers moved. There was a wariness to their steps, their eyes flickering toward the forest as though it were a living thing. Even the children stayed close to the adults, their laughter subdued.

Ethan stopped outside a small café, its faded sign swinging in the breeze. This is the place, he said, glancing at Lena. His expression was tense, his knuckles white as he gripped the journal.

How can you be sure? Lena asked, though her own pulse quickened as she took in the quaint building. The journal's description had been vague, but something about the place felt… familiar.

Ethan flipped open the journal, pointing to a rough sketch of the café's facade. Look, he said. It's the same.

Lena nodded, her unease deepening. Okay, let's see what we can find.

Inside, the café was dimly lit and sparsely populated. The air smelled of brewed coffee and old wood, a mix of comfort and age. A few locals sat at scattered tables, their conversations quiet. They barely looked up as Lena and Ethan entered, but she felt their gazes linger when they thought she wasn't looking.

Behind the counter stood an elderly man with a lined face and sharp, knowing eyes. He wiped his hands on a towel and regarded them with a mixture of curiosity and suspicion. You're not from around here, he said, his voice gruff but not unkind.

No, Ethan said, stepping forward. We're just passing through. I was hoping you could help us.

The man raised an eyebrow. Help you with what?

Ethan hesitated, glancing at Lena before pulling the journal from under his arm. He opened it to one of the sketches of Elise and held it out. Have you seen her before?

The man's eyes narrowed as he leaned closer, his expression hardening. He stared at the sketch for a long moment, his fingers tightening around the towel in his hands. Where did you get this? he asked, his voice low.

It was in the cabin, Ethan said carefully. The one deeper in the forest. It belonged to my great-uncle.

The man's gaze snapped up to Ethan's, his eyes sharp. Your great-uncle… Ethan Gray?

Ethan nodded slowly, his jaw tightening. You knew him?

The man exhaled heavily, setting the towel aside. He gestured for them to follow him into a back room, his movements hurried. Come, he said. This isn't a conversation to have out here.

Lena exchanged a wary glance with Ethan but followed the man into the dimly lit back room. It was cluttered with papers, old photographs, and maps of the surrounding forest. The man closed the door behind them, leaning against it as though to guard against unseen eyes.

That woman, he said, nodding toward the journal in Ethan's hands. Elise. Everyone in this village remembers her.

Lena's heart raced. What happened to her?

The man hesitated, his gaze flickering toward the window as though expecting the forest itself to answer. She was… different, he said finally. Beautiful, kind, but there was always something about her. She didn't belong here—not in the way the rest of us did.

What do you mean? Ethan asked.

She wasn't meant to stay, the man said, his voice growing quieter. The forest doesn't like it when outsiders linger. It has its own rules, its own… balance.

Your great-uncle upset that balance when he brought her here.

And the mist? Lena pressed. What does it have to do with her?

The man's expression darkened. The mist is the forest's way of keeping its secrets. It takes what doesn't belong and hides it. Sometimes, it gives something back. But not always.

Lena's stomach twisted. Are you saying the mist took her?

The man didn't answer immediately. He walked to a small cabinet, rummaging through its contents before pulling out an old, faded photograph. He handed it to Ethan, his hands trembling slightly.

The photograph was black and white, the edges frayed. It showed a woman standing at the edge of the forest, her face partially obscured by the mist curling around her. Even in the grainy image, Lena recognized her immediately.

Elise, Ethan whispered.

The man nodded. That was the last time anyone saw her. She walked into the forest and never came out.

Lena's pulse quickened. And my resemblance to her? she asked, her voice trembling. People keep saying…

You look just like her, the man said bluntly. It's uncanny. Almost like she's come back.

Lena's chest tightened. She didn't know whether to feel flattered or terrified. Why would the forest bring her back? she asked, her voice barely above a whisper.

The man's gaze was heavy, his voice laced with warning. The forest doesn't forget. And it doesn't forgive.

A chill ran down Lena's spine. The room felt smaller, darker, as though the shadows themselves were closing in. She turned to Ethan, who was staring at the photograph with a mix of awe and dread.

What now? she asked.

Ethan's jaw tightened, and he tucked the journal and photograph under his arm. We keep going, he said. The answers are out there, and we're going to find them.

The man's warning echoed in Lena's mind as they left the café and stepped back into the forest's edge. The trees seemed to lean closer, the air colder, as though the forest itself was watching them.

And somewhere in the distance, the mist began to rise.

Eight

The Storm

The forest loomed taller and darker as the day stretched on, its edges blurring into an ominous haze. Lena's footsteps crunched against the underbrush as she and Ethan followed the faint trail leading toward the next location marked in the journal—a glen said to hold traces of Elise's last journey. The unease that had taken root in her chest refused to fade. She kept glancing over her shoulder, half-expecting the mist to rise from the shadows and coil around her ankles.

The air was thick with tension. Even Ethan, who had maintained a stoic calm throughout the day, seemed more withdrawn. His eyes darted toward the canopy above every few minutes, as though he could sense something watching them.

We should stop soon, Lena said, her voice cutting through the eerie silence.

Ethan glanced at her, his brow furrowed. We're close. Another mile, maybe.

The light's fading, Lena pointed out. And the forest isn't exactly friendly at night.

Before Ethan could respond, a low rumble echoed through the trees. Lena froze, her gaze snapping to the sky. The clouds, once a dull gray, had darkened into a swirling mass of charcoal, their edges tinged with an unnatural green. Another rumble followed, louder this time, and a gust of wind swept through the forest, scattering leaves and sending a chill down Lena's spine.

We need to find shelter, Ethan said, his voice tense. He grabbed her arm, guiding her back down the trail.

The wind picked up, howling through the trees like a living thing. Lena clutched her coat tightly around her, the temperature dropping sharply. The forest seemed to shift around them, the trail disappearing into the shadows as the first drops of rain splattered against the ground.

There! Ethan shouted over the rising wind, pointing to a structure barely visible through the dense trees.

Lena followed him, her heart racing as they approached the dilapidated building. It was an old inn, its wooden walls warped with age and the windows boarded up haphazardly. The sign above the door hung at an awkward angle, the name long since faded.

Ethan pushed the door open, the hinges creaking in protest. The inside was dark and musty, the air thick with the scent of damp wood. They stumbled into the main room, their breaths visible in the cold air.

This place is barely standing, Lena said, her voice shaky.

It's better than being out there, Ethan replied, gesturing to the storm raging outside.

They lit a small lantern Ethan had in his pack, its faint glow casting long shadows across the room. The space was sparse, with a few broken chairs and a crumbling fireplace. Lena shivered as the wind howled outside, rattling the walls.

As they settled against the far wall, Ethan unrolled his coat, spreading it across the floor for them to sit on. The journal sat between them, its leather cover glinting faintly in the lantern light.

We should keep reading, Lena said, her voice soft. There might be something we missed.

Ethan nodded, flipping through the pages until he found an entry that matched the map's description of the glen. He read aloud, his voice steady despite the storm raging around them.

July 8th, 1973

Elise laughed as she stepped into the glen, the mist swirling around her ankles like a playful child. I wanted to pull her back, to keep her safe, but she was fearless. She said the glen held secrets, that if we listened closely, the mist would speak to us. I think it already has.

Ethan's voice faltered, his gaze lingering on the page. She wasn't afraid, he murmured.

Lena leaned closer, her fingers brushing against the worn edges of the journal. Maybe she should have been.

Before Ethan could respond, a loud crack of thunder shook the inn, and the lantern flickered violently. The air grew colder, the light casting shifting shadows across the walls.

Lena's breath hitched as a faint whisper reached her ears. It was soft, barely audible, but unmistakable. She turned toward the boarded-up window, her pulse quickening.

Did you hear that? she whispered.

Ethan tensed, his gaze following hers. Hear what?

Lena strained her ears, but the sound was gone, swallowed by the storm. She shook her head, trying to steady her breathing. It's nothing. Just the wind.

But deep down, she knew better.

Nine

A Forgotten Portrait

The small gallery smelled faintly of varnish and aging wood. Its walls, lined with muted gray paint, displayed an array of oil paintings, charcoal sketches, and watercolors that spoke of forgotten memories and faded histories. Lena stepped inside cautiously, her gaze sweeping over the room. Ethan was already several paces ahead, his camera slung over his shoulder as he examined a series of black-and-white photographs.

Isn't this incredible? he asked over his shoulder, his voice low but filled with curiosity. It's like a time capsule of the town's past.

Lena nodded absently, her attention snagged by a collection of portraits on the far wall. They were delicate, rendered in soft hues that contrasted sharply with the bold, surreal landscapes that dominated the gallery. The faces in the portraits were haunting, their expressions suspended between serenity and sorrow.

As she approached the wall, a particular portrait caught her eye. It was tucked into a corner, unassuming and nearly obscured by the more prominent works around it. The woman in the painting had dark hair that cascaded over her shoulders, her eyes deep and reflective, as though she were holding a thousand unspoken secrets.

Lena's breath caught in her throat. The woman in the portrait looked exactly like her.

Her steps faltered, the gallery's quiet hum fading into silence. She leaned closer, her eyes scanning every detail—the curve of the woman's lips, the soft shadow under her cheekbone, the way her gaze seemed to follow Lena wherever she moved. It was uncanny, as though she were staring into a mirror that reflected a version of herself she had never met.

Ethan, she called out, her voice trembling. Come here.

He appeared at her side within moments, his brow furrowing as he followed her gaze. What is it? he asked.

Lena pointed to the portrait, her hand shaking slightly. Look.

Ethan's eyes widened as he took in the painting. That's… His voice trailed off, his expression shifting from confusion to unease. That's impossible.

I know, Lena whispered. But it's her. It's me.

Ethan stepped closer, his fingers brushing against the small plaque beneath the portrait. The name listed was simple, almost cryptic: *E.G.*. Below it was a date: fifty years ago.

E.G., Ethan murmured, his mind racing. That's… those are my initials.

Lena turned to him, her chest tightening. You think you painted this?

No, Ethan said quickly, shaking his head. I mean, I couldn't have. I wasn't even alive fifty years ago. But… someone in my family could have. My great-uncle, maybe. He was an artist.

Lena's fingers brushed against the edge of the frame, her thoughts spiraling. Do you think he knew her? The woman in the journal? Elise?

Ethan frowned, his gaze lingering on the portrait. Maybe. It would explain why this feels so familiar. Why I feel so… connected to this place.

Lena took a step back, her mind racing. But why does she look like me? she asked, her voice barely above a whisper. This isn't just resemblance, Ethan. It's exact. The same eyes, the same hair… even the same expression.

Ethan didn't respond immediately. He stared at the portrait, his jaw tightening. I don't know, he said finally, his voice low. But I'm going to find out.

Before Lena could press him further, a gallery attendant approached, her footsteps soft against the wooden floor. It's beautiful, isn't it? the woman said, her smile kind but distant. One of our oldest pieces.

Lena turned to her, her heart pounding. Do you know anything about the artist? she asked.

The attendant nodded. Not much, I'm afraid, she said. The artist was very private. We only know his initials—E.G.—and that he lived in the area for a time. The painting was donated decades ago by a local family.

What about the woman in the portrait? Ethan asked, his tone sharper than he intended. Do you know who she was?

The attendant hesitated, her gaze flickering to the portrait. There are rumors, she said cautiously. Some say she was his muse. Others say she was…

something more. But no one knows for sure. The records are incomplete.

Lena exchanged a glance with Ethan, her unease growing. Thank you, she said quietly, her voice trembling. The attendant nodded and walked away, leaving them alone with the painting.

Ethan stepped closer to the portrait, his fingers brushing against the frame. This isn't a coincidence, he said, his voice steady but laced with tension. This is connected to the journal, to the cabin... to everything.

Lena's chest tightened as she stared at the woman's face. Her face. What do we do now? she asked, her voice barely audible.

Ethan turned to her, his dark eyes filled with determination. We keep looking, he said. There's more to this story, and I'm not stopping until we find the truth.

As they turned to leave, Lena cast one last glance at the portrait. The woman's gaze seemed to follow her, as though silently urging her forward. The weight of the mystery pressed against her chest, heavy and unrelenting. Whatever lay ahead, she knew they were only beginning to uncover the secrets of the past.

Ten

Dreams of Elise

The night after their discovery at the gallery was restless. Lena lay on the small bed in the cabin, staring at the ceiling as moonlight spilled through the cracked window, casting pale shadows that danced across the room. Her mind was a storm of questions, none of which seemed to have answers. The woman in the portrait haunted her thoughts, her familiar face a riddle she couldn't solve.

Lena shifted under the blanket, her chest tightening as a strange sensation settled over her. The air felt heavy, charged with an energy that prickled her skin. She turned her head toward the window, half-expecting to see something—or someone—watching her from the forest beyond. But there was nothing, only the faint rustle of leaves in the cool night breeze.

Eventually, exhaustion claimed her, and she slipped into a restless sleep.

—-

The dream began in darkness. At first, it was formless, a swirling void that pressed against her senses. Then, slowly, shapes began to emerge—a forest bathed in twilight, the trees twisting and bending unnaturally as though alive. The air was thick with mist, curling around her feet and rising like ghostly tendrils.

Lena walked forward, her steps soundless on the forest floor. She didn't know where she was going, but something pulled her onward, a force both foreign and familiar. The whispers started softly, threading through the air like a distant melody.

Lena...

The sound of her name sent a chill down her spine. She turned, her heart pounding, but the forest behind her was empty.

Who's there? she called out, her voice trembling. The whispers grew louder, overlapping into a chaotic symphony that seemed to come from everywhere and nowhere.

Come to me.

The voice was soft, almost pleading, and unmistakably female. Lena's chest tightened as the mist parted ahead of her, revealing a figure standing in the distance. She was tall and slender, her dark hair cascading over her shoulders like a waterfall of ink. Her face was obscured by shadow, but Lena didn't need to see it to know who she was.

Elise, she whispered, her voice barely audible.

The figure didn't respond. Instead, she turned and began walking deeper into the forest, her movements graceful but deliberate. The mist swirled around her, obscuring her form with each step.

Wait! Lena called, breaking into a run. The forest seemed to close in around her, the trees leaning toward her as though trying to stop her. The whispers grew louder, filling her ears and pressing against her thoughts.

Don't follow.

Stay away.

You will lose yourself.

But Lena ignored the warnings, her focus fixed on the figure ahead. She pushed through the thickening mist, her breath coming in sharp gasps as the forest grew darker. The whispers shifted, becoming more urgent, more desperate.

She disappeared into the mist...

The words sent a chill through Lena, but she didn't stop. She stumbled into a clearing, her steps faltering as the figure came into view once more. Elise stood at the center, her back to Lena, her form shrouded in mist. The ancient tree loomed behind her, its roots twisting into the earth like veins, its bark glowing faintly with strange, otherworldly runes.

Elise, Lena said, her voice trembling. Who are you? Why do I see you everywhere?

The figure turned slowly, and Lena's breath caught in her throat. Elise's face was identical to her own, down to the curve of her lips and the shadows under her eyes. But where Lena's expression was filled with fear and confusion, Elise's was calm, almost serene.

You know me, Elise said softly, her voice carrying a haunting familiarity. You've always known me.

Lena shook her head, her hands trembling at her sides. I don't understand, she said. Why do I look like you? What does this mean?

Elise stepped closer, her gaze piercing. Because you are me, she said, her voice steady. And I am you.

Lena's chest tightened, her mind racing. That's impossible, she said, her voice breaking. I'm not you. I've never even been to this place before.

Elise tilted her head, her expression unreadable. Haven't you? she asked. Or have you simply forgotten?

Before Lena could respond, the whispers surged, louder and more chaotic than ever. The ground trembled beneath her feet, and the mist thickened, curling around her like chains. Elise's form began to fade, her features dissolving into the haze.

No! Lena shouted, reaching out toward her. Don't go! I need answers!

Elise's voice echoed through the clearing, soft and distant. The answers lie within you, Lena. But be careful what you seek. The truth can be dangerous.

The mist surged upward, swallowing the clearing in an instant. Lena felt herself falling, the ground giving way beneath her as the whispers reached a deafening crescendo.

—-

Lena woke with a start, her breath coming in ragged gasps. The cabin was silent, the first rays of dawn filtering through the window. Her heart pounded as she sat up, her hands clutching the blanket tightly.

Ethan was already awake, seated at the table with the journal open before him. He looked up as she stirred, his expression filled with concern.

Lena, he said softly. Are you okay?

She shook her head, her voice trembling. I saw her, she said. In my dreams. Elise. She… she told me I already know the answers. That the truth is inside me.

Ethan's brow furrowed, and he set the journal aside. What do you think she meant?

I don't know, Lena admitted, her voice breaking. But I'm scared, Ethan. What if… what if this is more than just a connection? What if I really am her?

Ethan crossed the room, his hand resting gently on her shoulder. Whatever this is, he said, his voice steady, we'll figure it out. Together.

Lena nodded, her tears falling silently. But as she glanced at the journal and the photograph of Elise on the table, a deep unease settled over her. The whispers from the dream lingered in her mind, a chilling reminder of the danger that lay ahead.

Eleven

The Midnight Chase

The forest was alive in the dead of night. The trees swayed in a wind that didn't reach the ground, and the mist curled around the edges of the campfire, flickering like ghostly tendrils. Lena sat with her knees drawn to her chest, unable to shake the feeling that she was being watched. Across from her, Ethan had fallen into a restless sleep, his features tense even in repose.

The dream still lingered in Lena's mind, a haunting echo of Elise's piercing eyes and the whispered words: *You must remember.* She shivered and pulled her coat tighter around her shoulders, though the chill that enveloped her wasn't from the night air.

Then she saw it.

A shadow, barely perceptible, moved between the trees just beyond the firelight. It was subtle at first—a flicker in the corner of her eye. But as she stared, the figure grew clearer. It was tall, unmistakably human, and its movements were deliberate.

Ethan, she whispered, her voice trembling.

He didn't stir.

The shadow moved again, stepping into the faint glow of the fire. Her breath caught in her throat as she recognized the figure. It was Ethan—or at least, it looked like him. But his features were blurred, his eyes hollow and dark.

Ethan! she hissed, louder this time.

The real Ethan bolted upright, his hand instinctively reaching for the lantern. What is it? he asked, his voice sharp.

Lena pointed toward the figure, but it had disappeared into the shadows. It was you, she said, her voice shaking. I saw you—walking into the forest.

Ethan's brow furrowed. He grabbed the lantern and stood, his gaze scanning the treeline. Are you sure?

Yes, Lena said, standing as well. It was you. Or… something that looked like you.

The mist thickened, creeping closer to their camp. Ethan lit the lantern, the warm glow cutting through the darkness, but the sense of unease remained. Stay here, he said, his tone firm.

Like hell I will, Lena shot back, grabbing her coat. I'm not letting you go out there alone.

Ethan didn't argue. Together, they ventured into the forest, the lantern casting long, shifting shadows. The silence was deafening, broken only by the crunch of leaves underfoot. The mist seemed to part for them, only to close in again once they passed.

Do you see anything? Lena whispered, her voice barely audible.

Ethan shook his head, his jaw clenched. No, but something's—

He stopped abruptly, holding up a hand. Lena followed his gaze and felt her blood run cold. In the distance, the shadowy figure reappeared, standing perfectly still. This time, there was no mistaking it—it was identical to Ethan, down to the clothes he wore.

What the hell… Ethan murmured.

The figure tilted its head, as if studying them, before turning and walking deeper into the forest. Ethan took a step forward, but Lena grabbed his arm.

Don't, she said, her voice shaking. It's leading us somewhere.

I know, Ethan said grimly. And we need to find out why.

Against her better judgment, Lena followed him as he pursued the figure. The trees grew denser, the mist thicker, until the lantern's light barely illuminated the path ahead. The figure remained just out of reach, always disappearing around a corner or behind a tree.

Finally, they emerged into a small clearing. The figure was gone, but at the center of the space stood the cabin.

No, Lena whispered, her heart sinking. How did we get back here?

Ethan looked as bewildered as she felt. We followed it, he said, his voice low. It led us here.

Lena took a step toward the cabin, her pulse quickening. The air was heavy, charged with an almost electric energy. Why?

Ethan didn't answer. He approached the cabin's door, pushing it open with a creak. The interior was exactly as they had left it—dusty, cold, and filled with the echoes of the past. But something was different.

On the table where they had left the journal, another object now rested. It was a photograph, its edges yellowed with age. Ethan picked it up, his hands trembling slightly.

It's her, he said softly.

Lena peered over his shoulder. The photograph showed Elise standing in the glen, her expression serene. But behind her, the mist swirled unnaturally, forming the faint outline of a figure.

Who's that? Lena asked, her voice barely audible.

Ethan shook his head. I don't know. But I think we're supposed to find out.

Twelve

The Mist

The photograph was impossibly vivid for its age, the image so sharp that Lena could see the fine details in Elise's flowing dress. Her eyes, filled with quiet determination, seemed to bore into Lena's very soul. But it was the figure in the mist behind her that held her attention. Though faint, it exuded a presence that felt oppressive and watchful.

Why would this be here? Lena asked, her voice trembling as she stared at the photograph.

Ethan's jaw tightened. It's another piece of the puzzle, he said, though his tone lacked confidence. He placed the photograph gently on the table beside the journal. The mist keeps leading us back here. There's something it wants us to see.

Lena shivered, glancing out the broken window. The mist outside had grown thicker, curling around the cabin like a living thing. What if it doesn't want us to see anything? What if it's trying to trap us?

Ethan didn't respond immediately. He walked to the window, his hand resting on the worn sill as he stared into the shifting haze. If it wanted to trap us, it would have already done it, he said finally. I think… I think it's trying to tell us something.

Tell us what? Lena asked, frustration creeping into her voice. It's a mist, Ethan. It's not exactly great at communication.

Before Ethan could reply, a loud creak echoed through the cabin. Both of them froze, their gazes snapping to the door. The wind howled outside, but the door remained shut.

Did you hear that? Lena whispered, her heart pounding.

Ethan nodded, his expression grim. Stay here.

Like hell I will, Lena said, grabbing the lantern from the table. If you're going out there, I'm coming with you.

Ethan didn't argue. He grabbed a flashlight from his bag, and together they stepped outside. The cold night air hit Lena like a slap, and the mist enveloped them instantly, its damp tendrils clinging to her skin. The lantern's glow was weak against the haze, barely illuminating the ground beneath their feet.

Do you see anything? Lena asked, her voice barely audible over the sound of the wind.

Ethan shook his head. No, but something's—

He stopped abruptly, his flashlight beam cutting through the mist to reveal a faint silhouette. It stood a few feet away, motionless and indistinct, its edges blurred by the swirling haze.

Lena's breath caught in her throat. Is that…?

Ethan stepped closer, his movements slow and deliberate. Stay back, he said, his voice low.

The silhouette didn't move as Ethan approached. His flashlight revealed more details—a figure in a long dress, its back turned to them. The fabric of the dress rippled as though caught in an invisible breeze.

It's her, Ethan said, his voice barely above a whisper.

Elise? Lena asked, her heart pounding.

The figure turned slowly, and Lena's stomach twisted in fear. The face was Elise's, but it wasn't quite right. Her features were sharper, almost distorted, and her eyes glowed faintly in the dim light.

Ethan, Lena said urgently, pulling him back. That's not her.

The figure tilted its head, studying them with an eerie stillness. Then it raised one hand and pointed toward the forest. The movement was fluid but unnatural, as though it were mimicking a human gesture.

Ethan's grip tightened on the flashlight. It's showing us something.

Or luring us, Lena countered, her voice shaking. Don't go.

But Ethan was already moving, drawn toward the figure as though in a trance. Lena hesitated for a moment before following him, the lantern's glow barely cutting through the thickening mist. The figure remained ahead of them, always just out of reach, its movements silent and deliberate.

They walked for what felt like hours, the forest around them growing darker and more oppressive. The trees seemed to close in, their gnarled branches reaching down like claws. Lena's legs ached, but she didn't dare stop. The mist grew denser, and the air grew colder with each step.

Finally, the figure stopped. They had entered a clearing, the trees forming a perfect circle around a shallow pool of water. The surface of the pool was unnaturally still, reflecting the faint glow of the mist like a mirror.

The figure stood at the edge of the pool, its gaze fixed on the water. Then, without warning, it stepped forward and dissolved into the mist, leaving nothing behind.

What the hell was that? Lena whispered, her voice trembling.

Ethan didn't answer. He approached the pool cautiously, his flashlight beam illuminating its surface. Lena followed, her heart racing as she stared into the water.

At first, it seemed empty, just a shallow pool of clear water. But as they stared, shapes began to form beneath the surface. Shadows moved like tendrils, swirling and shifting into patterns that seemed almost human.

Do you see that? Lena asked, her voice barely audible.

Ethan nodded, his expression tense. It's showing us something.

The shadows coalesced into a single image—a man and a woman standing at the edge of a forest. The man's face was obscured, but the woman's was unmistakably Elise's. The mist swirled around them, growing thicker and darker until it consumed them completely.

Then the image changed. The shadows became violent, twisting into clawed shapes that lashed out at the couple. The man raised his arms as though trying to shield Elise, but the mist overwhelmed them both.

The water stilled, and the image disappeared. Lena took a shaky step back, her legs threatening to give out. What… what does that mean?

Ethan's jaw tightened. It's their story, he said. Elise and my great-uncle. The mist took them.

And now it's coming for us, Lena said, her voice breaking.

Ethan turned to her, his eyes dark. Not if we stop it.

Thirteen

The Stranger

The walk back to the cabin was fraught with silence, the air heavy with the weight of what they had seen in the pool. The mist seemed to linger closer now, curling around their legs like a predator stalking its prey. Lena gripped the lantern tightly, its weak light barely piercing the darkness. Beside her, Ethan's expression was grim, his flashlight beam scanning the shadows as if expecting the figure to reappear.

When they reached the cabin, Lena dropped onto the nearest chair, her body trembling from a mixture of exhaustion and fear. Ethan placed the photograph and journal back on the table, his movements deliberate but tense. The soft creak of the floorboards beneath his feet was the only sound in the room.

We can't keep doing this, Lena said finally, her voice cracking. The mist isn't just showing us the past. It's trying to pull us into it.

Ethan leaned against the table, his hands braced on the worn wood. I know, he said quietly. But if we stop now, we'll never understand why it's doing this—or how to stop it.

Lena opened her mouth to respond, but a sudden knock at the cabin door froze the words in her throat. Her eyes snapped to Ethan, who stood straighter, his hand instinctively reaching for the flashlight.

Who the hell…? Ethan murmured, his voice low.

The knock came again, louder this time. It was deliberate, forceful, and far too human for the eerie stillness of the forest. Lena stood, her pulse racing as Ethan crossed the room and opened the door.

A man stood on the porch, his silhouette framed by the faint glow of the lantern light. He was tall and lean, his features sharp and weathered, as though he had spent years braving the harsh elements of the forest. His eyes, a piercing gray, scanned the cabin's interior before settling on Ethan.

You're Ethan Gray, the man said, his voice low and rough, as though he hadn't spoken in days.

Ethan's brow furrowed. Who are you?

The man stepped inside without waiting for an invitation, his boots thudding against the floor. Victor, he said simply. I knew your great-uncle.

Lena exchanged a wary glance with Ethan before stepping forward. How did you find us? she asked, her voice sharp.

Victor's gaze shifted to her, his gray eyes cold and calculating. The mist led me, he said. It always does.

Ethan stepped between Lena and Victor, his posture defensive. What do you want?

Victor sighed, rubbing a hand over his stubbled jaw. To warn you, he said.

You're playing a dangerous game here. The mist doesn't like to be disturbed.

Ethan's jaw tightened. We're not disturbing it. We're trying to understand it.

Victor's expression darkened. There's nothing to understand, he said. The mist takes what it wants. It always has. It always will.

Why? Lena asked, stepping around Ethan. What does it want? Why did it take Elise?

Victor hesitated, his gaze flickering to the photograph on the table. He walked over to it, his fingers brushing the edge of the worn frame. Elise... he murmured. She was special. The forest knew that. The mist doesn't just take—it binds. It claimed her because she was different.

What do you mean 'different'? Ethan asked, his voice rising. She was just a person.

Victor turned to face them, his expression grim. She wasn't just anything, he said. The mist... it's alive. It feeds on those who don't belong. Those who stand out. And Elise stood out.

Lena's stomach twisted. And now it's coming for us.

Victor nodded slowly. Because you're following her path. The mist doesn't forget, and it doesn't forgive. It thinks you're trying to take her place.

Ethan stepped closer, his fists clenched at his sides. Then how do we stop it? How do we break this... this curse?

Victor's lips pressed into a thin line. You don't, he said. Not without a cost.

What kind of cost? Lena asked, her voice trembling.

Victor's gaze softened slightly as he looked at her, his tone gentler. The mist binds what it takes. To break that bond, you'd have to give it something in return. A trade.

Lena's chest tightened. A soul.

Victor nodded. It's the only way.

Ethan shook his head, his voice hard. There has to be another way.

If there was, don't you think your great-uncle would have found it? Victor snapped, his voice sharp. He spent years trying to save her, and it got him nothing but grief.

Ethan's hands trembled, his fists unclenching. He loved her, he said quietly. He wouldn't have given up.

And neither should we, Lena added, her voice steady despite the fear swirling in her chest. There has to be another way.

Victor sighed, his shoulders slumping. You're both stubborn. Just like him. He turned toward the door, his hand resting on the handle. If you want to keep going, I won't stop you. But don't say I didn't warn you.

Why do you care? Ethan asked, his voice laced with suspicion.

Victor paused, his back still to them. Because I've seen what the mist can do, he said. And I wouldn't wish it on anyone.

With that, he opened the door and stepped out into the night, disappearing into the mist as though he had never been there at all.

Fourteen

Unraveling the Truth

Victor's departure left the cabin in an oppressive silence. The door creaked closed, and Lena and Ethan exchanged uneasy glances. The weight of Victor's warning hung heavily in the air, his words echoing in Lena's mind: The mist binds what it takes. To break that bond, you'd have to give it something in return.

Lena sat down heavily at the table, staring at the photograph of Elise. Her serene face felt like a mockery of their current turmoil. Do you think he's right? she asked, her voice trembling. That there's no way to stop this without… without a trade?

Ethan didn't respond immediately. He paced the room, his jaw tight and his fists clenching and unclenching. I don't know, he said finally. But I'm not about to let the mist take you—or anyone else.

Lena's chest tightened at the raw determination in his voice. And what if it tries to take you? she asked, her voice barely above a whisper.

Ethan stopped pacing and looked at her, his dark eyes unreadable. Then we figure this out before it comes to that.

Lena nodded, though her fear didn't abate. She picked up the journal, flipping through its pages with trembling hands. There has to be something in here, she murmured. Something we missed.

As she scanned the journal, a phrase leaped out at her from one of the earlier entries:

—-

The glen holds its secrets, but the forest hides its truth. If we want answers, we must go where the mist is strongest.

—-

Ethan, Lena said, her voice sharp. Look at this.

He crossed the room and leaned over her shoulder, his brow furrowing as he read the passage. The glen, he said, his voice thoughtful. That's where we saw the pool.

Do you think it's talking about the pool? Lena asked. Or is there something else we missed?

Ethan straightened, his gaze distant. The mist was stronger near the pool, he said. It showed us something there—something it wanted us to see. Maybe it's trying to guide us.

Or manipulate us, Lena countered, closing the journal. Victor said the mist doesn't forget or forgive. What if it's setting a trap?

Ethan exhaled sharply, running a hand through his hair. It might be, he admitted. But we don't have a choice. If we don't follow the trail, we'll never understand what it wants—or how to stop it.

Lena swallowed hard, her stomach twisting with fear. Then we go back to the glen, she said, her voice trembling. But we have to be careful.

Ethan nodded, grabbing his flashlight and the journal. Careful doesn't even begin to cover it.

—-

The walk to the glen was shrouded in an unnatural stillness. The forest seemed to watch them, its towering trees casting long, distorted shadows across the ground. The mist lingered at the edges of their vision, curling and shifting like it was alive.

When they reached the glen, Lena felt a chill run down her spine. The pool at the center was still, its surface reflecting the faint light of the moon. The air was heavy, the silence deafening.

Do you feel that? Lena whispered.

Ethan nodded, his flashlight beam sweeping across the clearing. It's like the air is… waiting.

They approached the pool cautiously, their footsteps muffled by the soft ground. As they reached the edge, Lena noticed something she hadn't seen before—a faint glow emanating from beneath the water.

What is that? she asked, her voice trembling.

Ethan knelt at the edge, peering into the pool. It looks like… writing, he said, his tone filled with disbelief.

Lena crouched beside him, her heart pounding as she stared into the water. Sure enough, faint words were etched into the stone beneath the surface, glowing with an otherworldly light.

To break the bond, one must give. The heart of the mist demands a soul to unbind what it holds.

Lena's breath hitched, and she stumbled back, her chest tightening. It's true, she said, her voice barely audible. What Victor said—it's true.

Ethan's jaw tightened. It's not the only way, he said firmly. There has to be another way.

Before Lena could respond, the mist surged around them, rising like a wave. The pool's surface rippled violently, and the glowing words disappeared. A low, guttural growl echoed through the glen, sending a chill down Lena's spine.

Ethan, she whispered, grabbing his arm. We need to leave.

But Ethan didn't move. His gaze was fixed on the pool, his expression hard. It's trying to scare us, he said. But we're not running.

The growl grew louder, and the mist began to take shape. A shadowy figure rose from the pool, its form shifting and indistinct. Its hollow eyes glowed faintly, and its voice was a low, guttural rumble.

You seek to unbind what cannot be undone. You do not belong here.

Lena's blood ran cold. She grabbed Ethan's arm, pulling him back. Ethan, we have to go. Now.

But Ethan held his ground, his flashlight beam cutting through the mist. What do you want? he demanded, his voice steady despite the fear in his eyes. Why are you doing this?

The figure didn't respond. It tilted its head, its glowing eyes fixed on Lena. *A soul for a soul. The bond must hold.*

No, Ethan said, stepping in front of Lena. You're not taking her.

The figure's form wavered, its eyes narrowing. *Then you will take her place.*

Lena's heart stopped. No! she shouted, stepping forward. You're not taking him either!

The figure let out a low, chilling laugh, the sound reverberating through the glen. The mist surged around them, and the growl rose to a deafening roar. Lena grabbed Ethan's hand, her grip tight.

Run! she shouted, pulling him toward the edge of the glen.

They sprinted through the forest, the mist chasing after them like a living thing. The shadows seemed to stretch and twist, reaching for them with clawed fingers. Lena's lungs burned, her legs trembling with every step, but she didn't stop.

When they finally reached the cabin, they slammed the door shut, collapsing against it. The mist howled outside, scratching at the windows like a feral beast.

Ethan turned to Lena, his breath ragged. This isn't over, he said, his voice grim. It's just beginning.

Fifteen

The Connection

The cabin's walls groaned as the mist pressed against them, its eerie tendrils visible through the cracked window panes. Lena leaned against the door, her chest heaving from their frantic escape. Ethan sat on the floor, his back against the table, gripping the journal as though it were a lifeline.

This thing isn't letting up, Lena said, her voice trembling. It knows we're getting closer.

Ethan nodded, his dark eyes fixed on the journal's frayed edges. That's why it's trying to scare us, he said, though his voice was tight with unease. The closer we get, the more desperate it becomes.

Lena shivered, rubbing her arms. Desperate to do what? Kill us? Take us?

Ethan shook his head. To stop us. To protect whatever it's hiding.

The weight of his words hung heavy in the room. Lena sank into one of the rickety chairs, her mind racing. She thought of the pool, of the glowing words etched into the stone. *A soul for a soul.* The phrase echoed in her mind, a chilling reminder of the price they might have to pay.

What if Victor was right? Lena asked softly, her voice barely above a whisper. What if there's no way to stop this without...

She couldn't finish the thought, but Ethan's expression hardened. There's another way, he said firmly. There has to be.

Lena wanted to believe him, but doubt gnawed at the edges of her resolve. She glanced at the photograph of Elise on the table, her serene face seeming almost mocking now. Why us? she asked, her voice trembling. Why did this start with them, and why is it pulling us in?

Ethan didn't answer immediately. He opened the journal, flipping through the pages until he found one of the sketches of Elise. The lines were delicate, capturing her likeness with haunting precision. Because we're connected, he said finally. Through them.

Lena frowned. You mean through your great-uncle?

Ethan nodded, but his expression was distant. Yes. But I think it's more than that. He hesitated, his fingers tracing the edge of the sketch. Do you remember what the villagers said? About you looking like Elise?

Lena's stomach twisted. How could I forget?

What if it's not just resemblance? Ethan said, his voice low. What if it's something deeper? What if the mist sees you as... her?

Lena's breath caught. The idea was absurd, yet it sent a chill through her. That's impossible, she said, shaking her head. I'm not her. I've never even been to this place until now.

But the dreams, Ethan said, his gaze sharp. You've been dreaming about her. About this place. About the mist.

Lena swallowed hard, her chest tightening. It's just my mind playing tricks on me.

Is it? Ethan pressed. Or is it the mist trying to reach you? To show you something?

Lena stood abruptly, pacing the small room. Even if that's true, what does it mean? That I'm supposed to… what? Finish what she started?

Ethan stood as well, crossing the room to place a hand on her shoulder. His touch was steady, grounding. I don't know, he admitted. But we need to figure it out. Together.

Lena looked up at him, her fear mirrored in his dark eyes. And if we can't?

Ethan's jaw tightened. We will.

A sudden knock at the door shattered the moment. Lena and Ethan froze, their gazes snapping to the entrance. The knock came again, louder this time, and the temperature in the room seemed to drop.

Who is it? Lena whispered, her voice trembling.

Ethan shook his head, motioning for her to stay back. He grabbed the flashlight from the table and approached the door cautiously. Who's there? he called out.

There was no answer. Only silence.

The knock came a third time, followed by the faint sound of a voice—low and muffled, as though carried by the wind. Help…

Lena's blood ran cold. Did you hear that?

Ethan nodded, his grip on the flashlight tightening. He opened the door a fraction, the weak beam of light cutting through the mist outside. A figure stood on the porch, hunched and trembling. It was a woman, her hair tangled and her clothes torn.

Help me, she said again, her voice barely audible.

Ethan opened the door wider, his expression a mix of suspicion and concern. Who are you? he asked.

The woman looked up, her face pale and gaunt. Her eyes were hollow, filled with a deep, unsettling emptiness. The mist, she said, her voice cracking. It's everywhere. It won't let me go.

Lena stepped closer, her fear warring with compassion. How did you get here? she asked.

The woman shook her head, her body trembling. I don't know. It keeps pulling me back.

Back where? Ethan pressed.

The woman's gaze darted to the forest, her voice dropping to a whisper. To the heart.

The words sent a chill through Lena. She stepped back, her chest tightening. What's at the heart? she asked, her voice barely audible.

The woman didn't answer. She took a step forward, her movements slow and deliberate. You shouldn't be here, she said, her voice taking on an unnatural edge. It will take you too.

Ethan stepped in front of Lena, his flashlight beam fixed on the woman. What are you talking about?

The woman's eyes darkened, her expression twisting into something inhuman. It's already begun, she said, her voice low and guttural. You can't stop it.

The mist surged forward, enveloping the porch and swallowing the woman whole. Lena stumbled back, a scream caught in her throat as the door slammed shut on its own. The cabin shook, the air thick with the sound of whispers.

Ethan grabbed her arm, pulling her away from the door. It's trying to scare us, he said, though his voice was tight with fear.

It's working, Lena whispered, clutching the photograph of Elise to her chest. The whispers grew louder, filling the room with a chaotic symphony.

And then, as suddenly as it had started, the mist retreated. The cabin fell silent, the air heavy with tension.

Lena turned to Ethan, her hands trembling. The heart, she said, her voice shaking. That's where it's leading us.

Ethan nodded, his expression grim. Then that's where we're going.

Sixteen

The Curse

The silence in the cabin was deafening, broken only by the faint crackle of the dying fire. Lena sat at the edge of the table, her hands clutching the photograph of Elise as though it might offer some kind of protection. Across from her, Ethan paced restlessly, his flashlight clutched tightly in his hand. His movements were sharp, his breathing uneven, as though the weight of their situation had finally become unbearable.

The heart, Lena murmured, her voice barely audible. She said the heart.

Ethan stopped mid-step and turned to face her. It's not just a place, he said, his jaw tight. It's the center of everything—the mist, the curse, whatever's binding it to this forest.

Lena's gaze dropped to the photograph in her hands. Elise's serene expression seemed hauntingly out of place now, a cruel reminder of the impossible task ahead. Victor said the mist binds what it takes, she said. If the heart is where it's strongest, then that's where the binding started.

Ethan nodded, but his expression darkened. And if that's where it started, it's probably where it ends.

Lena felt a chill run down her spine. The idea of venturing deeper into the forest, to the very source of the mist's power, filled her with dread. You're talking about breaking the curse, she said, her voice trembling. But Victor said—

I don't care what Victor said, Ethan snapped, his voice sharp. There has to be another way. A way that doesn't involve— He stopped, his hands clenching at his sides.

A soul, Lena finished for him, her voice barely above a whisper. A trade.

Ethan exhaled heavily, his shoulders slumping. We'll find another way, he said firmly. We have to.

Before Lena could respond, the journal on the table seemed to move on its own, its pages flipping wildly as though caught in an invisible wind. Both of them froze, their eyes fixed on the book as it finally stopped on a single page.

The words were scrawled in a different hand than the rest of the entries—harsher, more desperate:

—-

To bind is to take. To unbind is to give. But the forest does not forget. It demands payment, and it always collects.

—-

The air in the cabin grew colder, and the whispers returned, faint but insistent, threading through the silence like ghostly tendrils. Lena's chest tightened as she read the words, their meaning sinking in like a blade. It's warning us, she said, her voice trembling. Even if we find the heart, it won't let us leave.

Ethan's jaw tightened. He grabbed the journal, slamming it shut. Then we won't give it the chance.

Before Lena could protest, a loud knock echoed through the cabin. Both of them turned toward the door, their breath hitching. The knock came again, louder this time, followed by the sound of wood groaning as though under immense pressure.

Ethan, Lena whispered, fear gripping her chest. It's back.

He grabbed her arm, pulling her toward the far side of the room. Stay behind me.

The door creaked open slowly, and a cold gust of wind swept through the cabin. The lantern flickered, its weak light casting long, distorted shadows across the walls. A figure stepped inside, its movements unnaturally smooth. Lena's breath caught as she recognized it.

It was Elise.

Or rather, something that looked like her. The woman's features were sharper, her eyes glowing faintly with an unnatural light. She moved silently, her gaze fixed on Ethan.

You shouldn't be here, she said, her voice soft but hollow. The forest doesn't forgive.

Ethan took a step forward, his hand tightening around the flashlight. Why are you doing this? he demanded. Why won't you leave us alone?

The figure tilted its head, her expression unreadable. Because you're trying to break what cannot be broken, she said. The mist binds all it touches. You are no exception.

We're not giving up, Ethan said, his voice steady despite the tremor in his hands. Tell us how to stop it.

The figure's eyes darkened, her expression twisting into something colder. To unbind is to give, she said. A soul for a soul.

Lena stepped forward despite the fear coursing through her veins. There has to be another way, she said, her voice trembling. There has to be.

The figure's gaze shifted to her, and for a moment, its expression softened. The heart holds the truth, she said quietly. But the truth comes at a cost.

Before Lena could respond, the figure dissolved into mist, disappearing as suddenly as it had appeared. The cabin fell silent once more, the air thick with tension.

Ethan turned to Lena, his expression hard. We're going to the heart.

Ethan, wait, Lena said, grabbing his arm. What if it's a trap? What if the heart isn't the answer, but just… just another way for the mist to take us?

Then we'll face it together, Ethan said, his voice resolute. I'm not letting it win.

Lena wanted to argue, but the determination in his eyes silenced her. She nodded reluctantly, her fear warring with the faint hope that they might actually find a way to break the curse.

We leave at dawn, Ethan said, grabbing the journal and the flashlight. Get some rest. We'll need it.

—-

The night passed fitfully, the whispers haunting Lena's dreams with fragmented images of Elise and the mist. She woke before sunrise, her body trembling with unease. Ethan was already awake, standing by the window with the journal in his hands.

Ready? he asked, turning to face her.

Lena nodded, though her heart pounded in her chest. Ready.

Together, they stepped out into the mist-shrouded forest, the path ahead obscured by shadows. The whispers grew louder as they walked, their words a chilling promise of what lay ahead.

Seventeen

The Rift

The forest seemed alive as Lena and Ethan pressed deeper into its heart. The trees grew denser, their gnarled branches twisting together like skeletal fingers blocking out the weak morning sunlight. The mist thickened around them, curling along the forest floor and stretching toward their ankles like ghostly tendrils. Each step felt heavier, as though the forest itself was resisting their presence.

Lena clutched the journal tightly to her chest, her breaths shallow. The whispers had returned, faint but insistent, threading through the air like an invisible current. They weren't words she could understand—more like fragmented thoughts, distant and disjointed. She glanced at Ethan, who walked a few paces ahead, his flashlight beam cutting through the haze.

Do you hear it? she asked, her voice barely above a whisper.

Ethan nodded, his jaw tight. It's getting louder.

The trail they followed was barely visible, marked only by faint disturbances in the earth. It felt as though they were being guided—not by the journal, but by the forest itself. Lena's unease deepened with every step.

What if this is a trap? she asked, breaking the silence.

Ethan stopped and turned to face her. It doesn't matter, he said, his voice firm. We have to keep going.

But what if we're walking into exactly what it wants? Lena pressed. What if the heart isn't the answer but the end?

Ethan's expression softened slightly, and he stepped closer. Lena, he said, his voice quieter, we've come too far to stop now. If we don't do this, the mist will keep coming for us. For you.

Her chest tightened at the raw emotion in his voice. And if it takes you instead? she asked, her voice trembling. What then?

Ethan hesitated, his dark eyes searching hers. I won't let it, he said finally. I promise.

The promise felt fragile, like a thread stretched too thin, but Lena nodded, forcing herself to trust him. They continued in silence, the tension between them palpable.

—-

The forest grew darker as they approached a wide clearing. The mist was thicker here, swirling and shifting in unnatural patterns. At the center of the clearing stood an ancient tree, its massive trunk gnarled and scarred. The air around it seemed to hum with energy, and the whispers grew louder, overlapping into a chaotic chorus.

This has to be it, Ethan said, his voice barely audible over the whispers.

Lena stared at the tree, her heart pounding. It was unlike anything she'd ever seen, its roots twisting into the ground like veins, its bark etched with strange, glowing symbols. The mist seemed to emanate from the tree, curling around its base like smoke.

The heart, she murmured.

Ethan nodded, stepping toward the tree. The whispers grew louder, almost deafening, and Lena clutched her ears, trying to block out the sound. But the whispers weren't just external—they were inside her mind, pressing against her thoughts, trying to break through.

Give.

Take.

Bind.

Ethan, she said urgently, her voice trembling. Something's wrong.

He turned to her, his expression tense. Stay here, he said. I'll check it out.

No, Lena said firmly, grabbing his arm. We do this together.

Ethan hesitated, but the determination in her eyes silenced his protest. They stepped forward together, the ground beneath their feet soft and spongy as though it were alive. The air grew colder, and the symbols on the tree glowed brighter.

As they reached the base of the tree, a low rumble echoed through the clearing. The ground shook, and the mist surged upward, forming a towering figure. It was humanoid in shape, but its edges blurred and shifted like smoke. Its eyes glowed crimson, and its voice was a low, guttural growl.

You should not be here.

Ethan stepped in front of Lena, his flashlight beam fixed on the figure. We're not leaving until we end this, he said, his voice steady.

The figure tilted its head, its crimson eyes narrowing. *To unbind is to give. What will you offer?*

Ethan hesitated, his jaw tightening. There has to be another way, he said. We're not trading lives.

The figure let out a low, chilling laugh, the sound reverberating through the clearing. *There is no other way. The bond must hold.*

Lena stepped forward, her fear replaced by anger. Why? Why does the bond have to hold? What are you protecting?

The figure turned its glowing eyes on her, its form shifting slightly. *You do not understand. The bond is eternal. It cannot be broken without cost.*

Lena clenched her fists, her voice rising. Then tell us what happened to Elise! Tell us why she's part of this!

The figure hesitated, its form flickering. *Elise chose. She gave. The bond remains.*

Lena's breath hitched. She... she sacrificed herself?

She was taken, the figure said, its voice low. *The mist claimed her to preserve the bond.*

Ethan's hands clenched at his sides. Then take me, he said suddenly, his voice trembling with emotion. If that's what it takes to end this, then take me.

No! Lena shouted, grabbing his arm. You can't!

Ethan turned to her, his expression filled with pain. Lena, if it's the only way—

It's not, she said, her voice breaking. There has to be another way.

The figure watched them silently, its crimson eyes glowing brighter. *One must give. The bond must hold.*

The ground trembled again, and the whispers grew louder, pressing against Lena's mind like a vice. She clutched Ethan's arm, her chest tightening. Ethan, she said urgently. We need to figure this out before it's too late.

He nodded, his jaw tight. We will, he said, though his voice was laced with uncertainty.

The figure stepped closer, its form towering over them. *Decide*, it said, its voice echoing through the clearing. *Or be taken.*

Eighteen

The Warning

The figure loomed over them, its form rippling and shifting like smoke caught in a tempest. Its crimson eyes burned brighter, unblinking, as it waited for their response. The whispers grew louder, filling the clearing with a chaotic cacophony that made it hard to think. Lena's chest tightened as she clutched Ethan's arm, her breath shallow.

Ethan, she said, her voice trembling. We can't do this. There has to be another way.

Ethan didn't respond immediately. His jaw was tight, his dark eyes locked on the shadowy figure. If this thing wants a soul, it's not getting yours, he said firmly. That's not up for debate.

And it's not getting yours either, Lena shot back, her voice rising despite the fear threatening to overwhelm her. We're not playing by its rules.

The figure tilted its head, its glowing eyes narrowing. *The bond must hold*, it said, its voice echoing through the clearing. *There is no escape.*

Lena stepped forward, her fear replaced by a surge of defiance. Why? she demanded, her voice shaking but resolute. Why does the bond have to hold? What are you protecting?

The figure's form flickered, its edges blurring as though it were unraveling. The whispers faltered, breaking apart into fragments. For a moment, the air grew still, the oppressive weight lifting slightly.

The forest thrives on the bond, the figure said after a long silence. *To sever it is to destroy what remains.*

Lena frowned, her mind racing. What remains of what? The forest? The mist?

The bond sustains all, the figure said. *Without it, there is nothing.*

Ethan stepped forward, his flashlight beam cutting through the mist. Then why are you trying to destroy us? he demanded. If the bond is so important, why not leave us alone?

The figure's crimson eyes flared, its form solidifying. *You seek to unbind. The mist defends.*

Before Ethan could respond, the ground beneath them began to tremble. The tree at the center of the clearing glowed faintly, its symbols pulsing with an eerie light. The whispers returned, louder and more frantic, filling Lena's mind with disjointed thoughts.

Ethan! she cried, clutching her head. It's too much!

He grabbed her hand, his grip firm. We're leaving, he said, his voice resolute.

The figure didn't move as they backed away, its glowing eyes fixed on them.

Run, it said, its voice low and chilling. *But the mist will follow.*

—-

They didn't stop running until they reached the cabin, their breaths coming in ragged gasps. The forest seemed to close in around them, the mist curling along the edges of their vision. Lena collapsed onto the floor, her heart pounding as she struggled to catch her breath.

This isn't working, she said, her voice breaking. We're just running in circles.

Ethan slammed the door shut and leaned against it, his chest heaving. We're not giving up, he said, his tone firm. We just need to figure out what it wants.

It already told us what it wants, Lena said, her voice rising. A soul. A trade. That's the only way.

There has to be another way, Ethan insisted, his dark eyes blazing. We're missing something.

Lena shook her head, tears streaming down her face. Ethan, we can't keep pretending this is something we can fix. This thing—it's not going to stop until it gets what it wants.

He knelt beside her, his hands gripping hers tightly. Lena, he said softly, look at me.

She met his gaze, her chest tightening at the determination in his eyes.

We're going to figure this out, he said, his voice steady. We've come too far to give up now.

Before Lena could respond, the whispers returned, threading through the air like a sinister melody. They were louder this time, more insistent, and Lena felt a chill run down her spine.

You cannot escape.

The bond must hold.

One must give.

The lantern flickered violently, casting long, distorted shadows across the walls. Lena's breath hitched as the temperature in the room plummeted. She turned toward the window, her heart pounding as she saw the mist pressing against the glass.

It's here, she whispered, her voice trembling.

Ethan grabbed the flashlight and turned toward the door. Stay behind me.

Before he could move, the whispers grew louder, their chaotic symphony breaking into a single, chilling voice.

If you dig too deep, you'll lose him.

Lena froze, her blood running cold. The voice was familiar, almost like her own, but twisted and hollow. She turned toward Ethan, who stood rigid, his flashlight beam fixed on the door.

Did you hear that? she asked, her voice shaking.

He nodded, his expression grim. It's trying to scare us.

But Lena wasn't so sure. The voice had felt too personal, too direct. She glanced at the journal on the table, its worn cover seeming to stare back at her. What if it's not just a warning? she murmured. What if it's... a promise?

Ethan turned to her, his jaw tightening. Then we don't give it the chance.

—-

The rest of the night passed in a tense silence, the whispers fading but never fully disappearing. Lena stayed close to Ethan, her mind racing with the voice's ominous warning. When dawn finally broke, the forest was eerily quiet, the mist lingering like a predator waiting to strike.

We need to keep moving, Ethan said, his voice cutting through the silence.

Lena nodded, though her fear hadn't abated. As they stepped outside, the whispers returned, faint and fragmented, threading through the trees.

And somewhere in the distance, the mist began to rise.

Nineteen

Betrayal

The morning sun fought to pierce the thick canopy of the forest, its weak rays doing little to dispel the ever-present mist that clung to the ground like a shroud. Lena followed Ethan closely as they moved deeper into the woods, the journal tucked tightly under her arm. The memory of the whispers from the night before still clawed at her thoughts: *If you dig too deep, you'll lose him.*

Ethan hadn't spoken much since they left the cabin, his jaw tight and his eyes scanning their surroundings with a mix of focus and unease. Lena could feel the tension between them, heavy and unspoken. She knew he was trying to protect her, but the weight of the mist's warning lingered, a shadow over every step they took.

You're quiet, Lena said softly, her voice breaking the silence.

Ethan didn't turn to look at her. Just thinking, he said curtly.

About what? she pressed, though she already knew the answer.

He stopped abruptly, turning to face her. His dark eyes were filled with a storm of emotions—fear, anger, and something she couldn't quite name. About how we're going to end this, he said, his voice low. About how we're going to make sure it doesn't take you.

Lena's chest tightened. Ethan, you can't—

I'm not letting it take you, he interrupted, his tone sharp. So don't even try to argue.

She opened her mouth to respond, but the words caught in her throat. The determination in his voice was unyielding, but it only made the weight of the mist's warning press harder against her. *If you dig too deep, you'll lose him.*

Before she could say anything, a faint sound reached their ears. It was distant but distinct—the soft rustle of leaves, the crunch of footsteps on the forest floor. Lena froze, her heart pounding as she scanned the trees.

Did you hear that? she whispered.

Ethan nodded, his hand tightening around the flashlight. Stay close.

They moved cautiously toward the sound, the forest growing darker and quieter with each step. The mist thickened, swirling around their feet like a living thing. The whispers returned, faint but insistent, threading through the air.

And then they saw him.

Victor stood at the edge of a clearing, his back to them. He was hunched over slightly, his shoulders rising and falling with labored breaths. The journal they'd left in the cabin was clutched in his hands, its worn leather cover catching the dim light.

Victor? Ethan called out, his voice sharp.

The man turned slowly, his gray eyes locking onto Ethan and Lena. There was something off about his expression—his face was gaunt, his skin pale, and his eyes… his eyes seemed darker, emptier.

You shouldn't have come, Victor said, his voice hollow.

What are you talking about? Ethan demanded, stepping closer. What are you doing here? And why do you have the journal?

Victor's lips pressed into a thin line. I warned you, he said. But you didn't listen. You kept pushing. And now…

He trailed off, his gaze shifting to Lena. A flicker of something—pity? Regret?—crossed his face before his expression hardened. Now it's too late.

Lena's stomach twisted. What do you mean? she asked, her voice trembling. What's too late?

Victor didn't answer. Instead, he held up the journal, his hands trembling slightly. The mist doesn't forget, he said. It doesn't forgive. And it doesn't let go.

Ethan took another step forward, his jaw clenched. Victor, put the journal down. Whatever you're doing—

I'm doing what needs to be done, Victor snapped, his voice rising. You don't understand what you're dealing with. The bond… it's too strong. It will consume you both if you let it.

Lena's breath hitched. You're trying to stop it, she said, realization dawning. But why?

Victor's eyes softened briefly as he looked at her. Because I've seen what it does, he said quietly. I've seen what it takes.

Ethan shook his head, his voice filled with disbelief. And you think betraying us is the answer? You think stealing the journal and running will fix anything?

It's not betrayal, Victor said sharply. It's survival.

The air in the clearing grew colder, and the mist thickened, curling around Victor's feet. The whispers grew louder, overlapping into a chaotic symphony that made Lena's head pound.

You don't have to do this, Lena said, stepping forward despite the fear coursing through her. We can stop this together. There has to be a way.

Victor's expression twisted with anger and despair. You don't get it, he said, his voice trembling. The mist doesn't stop. It doesn't care. The only way to break the bond is to give it what it wants.

Lena's blood ran cold. A soul, she whispered.

Victor nodded. If you won't do it, I will.

Before Ethan could stop him, Victor turned and ran, disappearing into the mist. The whispers rose to a deafening crescendo, and the ground trembled beneath their feet.

Victor! Ethan shouted, sprinting after him.

Ethan, wait! Lena cried, chasing after him. But the mist surged forward, cutting them off. Lena stumbled to a stop, her vision obscured by the swirling haze. Ethan! she shouted, her voice breaking.

The whispers grew louder, and the mist closed in around her. For a moment, she thought she saw Victor's silhouette in the distance, clutching the journal as he disappeared into the trees. And then she was alone.

Ethan! she screamed, her chest tightening with panic.

There was no response. Only the whispers, louder and more insistent, threading through her mind.

He is gone.

Lena fell to her knees, her hands trembling as tears streamed down her face. No, she whispered. No, he's not.

The mist swirled around her, its cold tendrils brushing against her skin. The whispers pressed against her thoughts, filling her mind with images of Ethan—his dark eyes, his determined expression, his unwavering strength.

You will lose him.

Lena's breath hitched, and she clutched the photograph of Elise to her chest. I'll find him, she said, her voice trembling but resolute. You won't take him from me.

The mist didn't respond, but the oppressive weight pressing against her mind remained. She pushed herself to her feet, her fists clenched as she stared into the haze.

I'm not giving up, she said, her voice steady. Not now. Not ever.

And with that, she stepped into the mist, determined to find Ethan—no matter what it cost her.

Twenty

The Return

The mist was alive. It pulsed and shifted as though it had a heartbeat, its tendrils curling around Lena's legs and arms like a predator testing its prey. Every step forward was a struggle, the air thick and cold, sapping her strength. The whispers were relentless now, their overlapping voices a chaotic symphony of half-formed words and unsettling truths.

He is gone.

You will fail.

The bond must hold.

Lena gritted her teeth, forcing herself to keep moving. The forest around her was unrecognizable, its once-familiar paths obscured by the swirling haze. The trees seemed to twist and lean, their branches clawing at the air. She clutched the photograph of Elise in one hand, its edges crumpled from her grip, and the faint warmth of the golden locket around her neck was her only comfort.

Ethan! she called out, her voice hoarse from shouting. The mist swallowed her words, carrying them away into the void. Ethan, answer me!

A faint rustle to her left made her freeze. She turned slowly, her heart pounding as she peered into the haze. The outline of a figure emerged, tall and broad-shouldered, but shrouded in shadows. Her breath caught, hope flaring in her chest.

Ethan? she whispered, taking a tentative step forward.

The figure didn't move, its edges flickering like a mirage. Lena's stomach twisted as the whispers grew louder, almost mocking.

Not him.

She took another step, her hand trembling as she reached for the flashlight at her side. The beam of light cut through the mist, revealing the figure's face—or lack thereof. Its features were blurred, indistinct, as though it were a hollow shell of a man.

Lena stumbled back, her breath hitching. What are you? she demanded, her voice shaking.

The figure tilted its head, its movements slow and deliberate. Then it spoke, its voice a low, guttural rumble that seemed to reverberate through her bones.

He is ours.

No, Lena said, shaking her head. You can't have him.

The figure didn't respond. It began to dissolve into the mist, its form scattering like smoke. Lena surged forward, her fear replaced by desperation.

Wait! she shouted. Where is he? Tell me where he is!

The mist swirled violently, and the figure disappeared completely. Lena dropped to her knees, her chest heaving as tears streamed down her face. The whispers pressed against her mind, relentless and suffocating.

He is lost.

You will fail.

The bond must hold.

No! Lena screamed, her voice cracking. She clutched the photograph to her chest, her tears falling onto its worn surface. I won't lose him. Do you hear me? I won't!

The whispers faltered, the chaotic symphony breaking into fragments. The mist seemed to hesitate, its movements slowing. For a moment, the oppressive weight lifted, and Lena felt a faint warmth spread through her chest.

The locket.

She reached for it instinctively, her fingers brushing against the smooth metal. Its warmth intensified, spreading through her like a lifeline. The whispers faded further, their voices retreating as though repelled by the light emanating from the locket.

Lena closed her eyes, clutching the locket tightly. Show me, she whispered. Show me where he is.

The warmth grew stronger, pulsing like a heartbeat. Lena opened her eyes, and the mist around her began to shift. The tendrils unraveled, forming a narrow path that stretched into the distance. The whispers were faint now, their chaotic rhythm broken.

Without hesitation, Lena followed the path, her steps steady despite the fear still clawing at her chest. The forest grew darker as she walked, the air colder, but the locket's warmth guided her, a beacon in the void.

Finally, she saw him.

Ethan was slumped against a tree, his body limp and his face pale. The mist curled around him like a predator savoring its prey, but the warmth of the locket seemed to push it back as Lena approached.

Ethan, she whispered, dropping to her knees beside him. She shook his shoulder gently, her hands trembling. Ethan, wake up. Please.

He didn't respond, his breathing shallow. Lena's chest tightened, and she clutched the locket in one hand, pressing it against his chest. You're not leaving me, she said fiercely, her voice breaking. Do you hear me? You're not.

The locket glowed faintly, its warmth spreading through Ethan's body. His eyelids fluttered, and a faint groan escaped his lips. Lena's breath hitched, tears streaming down her face as she cradled his head.

Ethan, she said softly, her voice trembling. It's me. You're okay.

His eyes opened slowly, dark and unfocused at first. Then they met hers, and a faint smile tugged at his lips. Lena, he murmured, his voice weak. You... found me.

Of course I did, she said, her tears falling freely. I'm not letting you go.

He tried to sit up, but his body trembled with the effort. Lena helped him, her arms steadying him as he leaned against her. The mist, he said, his voice barely audible. It… it almost…

I know, Lena said, her voice firm. But it didn't. You're here. We're here.

The mist around them shifted, its movements slower now, almost hesitant. The whispers were faint, retreating into the distance like a fading storm. Lena held Ethan tightly, her resolve hardening.

We're going to end this, she said, her voice steady. Together.

Ethan nodded weakly, his hand clutching hers. Together.

Twenty-One

The Vision

The forest was silent as Lena and Ethan sat beneath the massive, gnarled tree that had once seemed like a predator waiting to strike. The mist swirled at the edges of the clearing, hesitant and restrained, as though it was watching, waiting for the perfect moment to move.

Ethan leaned heavily against Lena, his breathing steady but shallow. His skin was pale, and his eyes were half-closed, dark circles shadowing them. She clutched the locket tightly, its faint warmth still pulsing against her palm. Whatever power it held had driven the mist back, but Lena could feel the tension in the air, the growing pressure of something unseen closing in around them.

We can't stay here, Lena whispered, her voice trembling. It's only a matter of time before it tries again.

Ethan stirred, his eyes flickering open. Where do we go? he asked weakly. It's everywhere.

Lena bit her lip, glancing at the journal lying open beside them. The cryptic entries and eerie sketches offered no clear answers, only fragments of a story they were still struggling to piece together.

The heart, she said finally, her voice steadier than she felt. The mist keeps leading us there. Maybe that's where we'll find what we need to stop this.

Ethan's gaze met hers, and for a moment, he looked like he wanted to argue. But then he nodded, his jaw tightening. If that's where this ends, he said, then we finish it.

Lena helped him to his feet, her arm wrapped around his waist as they began moving toward the heart of the forest. The path was barely visible, obscured by the ever-present mist and the thick undergrowth. Every step felt like a battle against the oppressive air, and the whispers, though faint, never fully disappeared.

—-

The path twisted and turned, leading them deeper into the forest until the trees grew so dense that their branches intertwined, blocking out the sunlight. The mist thickened, curling around them like tendrils of smoke. Lena's chest tightened as she clutched the locket, its warmth pulsing faintly against her skin.

Then, without warning, the whispers surged.

Remember.

See.

Choose.

Lena gasped, clutching her head as the voices filled her mind, louder and more insistent than ever. Her vision blurred, and the forest around her seemed to dissolve into a swirl of light and shadow.

Lena! Ethan's voice was distant, muffled, as though he were speaking from the other side of a thick wall.

The world shifted, and suddenly Lena was standing in a different forest—one that was brighter, softer, untouched by the oppressive mist. The air was warm, filled with the sound of birdsong and the faint rustle of leaves. She turned, her heart pounding, and froze.

Elise stood before her.

She was just as Lena had seen her in the photographs and sketches—tall and graceful, her long dark hair cascading over her shoulders like a waterfall of ink. But there was something different about her now, something alive and vibrant that the images hadn't captured.

Lena, Elise said softly, her voice carrying an ethereal quality. You came.

Lena's breath caught in her throat. I... I don't understand, she stammered. Where am I? How are you here?

Elise stepped closer, her expression calm but somber. You're at the edge of the bond, she said. The place where everything began—and where it will end.

Lena shook her head, her chest tightening. I don't understand. What is this bond? Why is the mist doing this?

Elise's gaze softened, and she reached out, her hand brushing against Lena's arm. The mist is a keeper of balance, she said. It binds those who defy the rules of this place—those who try to take what doesn't belong.

Defy the rules? Lena repeated, her voice rising. What rules? What did you do?

Elise's expression darkened, and she glanced toward the edge of the clearing. I loved, she said simply. And I was loved in return. But the forest saw it as a threat.

Lena's heart twisted. Ethan's great-uncle, she whispered. He loved you.

Elise nodded, her eyes glistening with unshed tears. And I loved him. But love wasn't enough to save us. The mist took me, bound me to the forest, to preserve its balance.

Lena's breath hitched. And now it's coming for us, she said, her voice trembling. It thinks we're like you.

Elise's gaze sharpened. Because you are, she said. The bond isn't just about the mist—it's about you, Lena. You and Ethan. Your connection is what brought you here, what awakened the bond.

Lena shook her head, panic rising in her chest. No. That's not true. We're just trying to figure this out, to stop it—

You can't stop it, Elise said, her voice firm. Not without a choice. The bond can only be broken by sacrifice.

Lena's stomach churned. A soul, she whispered. That's what the mist wants.

Elise nodded. It's the only way.

Lena stepped back, her head spinning. No, she said, her voice cracking. There has to be another way. We can't—

Elise! Ethan's voice broke through the haze, pulling Lena back to the present.

She blinked, and the vision dissolved, leaving her standing in the darkened forest once more. Ethan was beside her, his hands gripping her arms, his dark eyes filled with concern.

Lena, he said urgently. What happened? You just… froze.

She shook her head, tears streaming down her face. I saw her, she whispered. I saw Elise. She said… she said the bond can only be broken by a choice. A sacrifice.

Ethan's jaw tightened, and he pulled her close, his arms wrapping around her protectively. We'll find another way, he said, his voice steady. We'll figure this out.

But Lena wasn't sure if there was another way. The mist pressed closer, the whispers growing louder once more. The heart of the forest lay ahead, and with it, the final truth.

Twenty-Two

The Shadows

The forest's embrace tightened as Lena and Ethan moved deeper toward the heart of the mist. The path ahead seemed to fold in on itself, the dense canopy above blocking out any light. The air was cold and damp, heavy with the weight of whispers threading through the trees. The mist curled around their feet, thicker and more deliberate, as though it were alive and watching.

Lena clutched Ethan's arm tightly, her fingers trembling. It's closer now, she whispered, her breath visible in the freezing air. I can feel it.

Ethan nodded, his jaw clenched. So can I.

The locket around Lena's neck pulsed faintly, its warmth pushing back the chill that seemed to seep into her very bones. She held onto it like a lifeline, the memory of Elise's words echoing in her mind: *The bond can only be broken by a choice. A sacrifice.*

She glanced at Ethan, her chest tightening. The resolve in his eyes was clear—he had already made his choice. But Lena wasn't willing to lose him, not after everything they'd endured.

We have to keep moving, Ethan said, his voice steady despite the tension in his body. The heart can't be far.

Lena hesitated, fear clawing at her chest. And when we get there? she asked, her voice trembling. What then?

Ethan turned to her, his expression softening for the briefest moment. We end this, he said. Together.

The shadows began to shift as they neared the clearing. At first, they were subtle—a flicker in the corner of Lena's eye, a ripple in the mist that didn't seem natural. But soon, they became more distinct, more deliberate. Figures moved between the trees, their forms dark and distorted, their movements fluid yet unnatural.

Lena's breath hitched as one of the figures stepped into the faint light of Ethan's flashlight. It was tall and humanoid, but its features were blurred, its edges indistinct. Its eyes glowed faintly, twin orbs of crimson that seemed to pierce through the darkness.

Ethan, Lena whispered, her voice shaking. Do you see them?

He nodded, his grip tightening on the flashlight. I see them.

The figure tilted its head, its movements slow and deliberate. Then, without warning, it lunged forward, its form stretching unnaturally as it moved. Ethan shoved Lena behind him, the beam of his flashlight cutting through the mist and landing squarely on the figure.

The creature froze, its form flickering and wavering as though the light disrupted it. It let out a low, guttural growl before retreating into the shadows.

They don't like the light, Ethan said, his voice tense. Stay close.

Lena nodded, her hands trembling as she gripped the locket tightly. The warmth of the pendant seemed to push back the worst of the cold, but it did little to calm her racing heart.

As they continued, more figures emerged from the mist. They moved in unison, their crimson eyes glowing as they watched Lena and Ethan. The whispers grew louder, overlapping into a chaotic symphony that made it impossible to think.

You cannot escape.

The bond must hold.

One must give.

Lena stumbled, her head spinning as the voices pressed against her mind. Ethan caught her, his arm steadying her as she clutched her head.

Lena, he said urgently. Stay with me.

I can't… it's too much, she whispered, her voice breaking.

Ethan's jaw tightened, and he turned the flashlight on the nearest figure, the beam cutting through the mist like a blade. The creature recoiled, its form flickering and dissolving into the haze.

They're trying to break us, he said, his voice fierce. Don't let them. You're stronger than this.

Lena nodded weakly, her grip on the locket tightening. The whispers receded slightly, their chaotic rhythm faltering as the locket's warmth grew stronger.

Keep moving, Ethan said, his hand gripping hers. We're almost there.

The clearing came into view suddenly, as though the forest had parted to reveal it. At the center stood a massive, ancient tree, its gnarled roots twisting into the earth like veins. The mist swirled around its base, thick and heavy, and the air hummed with energy.

Lena's breath caught as she saw the shadows gathered around the tree. They moved in a slow, deliberate circle, their crimson eyes fixed on the heart of the clearing. The whispers were deafening now, their voices blending into a single, chilling command.

Give.

Ethan stepped forward, his flashlight beam sweeping across the clearing. The shadows faltered, their movements slowing, but they didn't retreat. The mist curled around his feet, tugging at him like invisible hands.

Lena, he said, his voice steady. Stay behind me.

No, she said, her voice trembling but firm. We do this together.

Ethan glanced at her, his expression conflicted, but he nodded. Together.

They stepped into the clearing, the locket around Lena's neck glowing faintly as the whispers reached a fever pitch. The shadows closed in, their movements quick and jerky, but they stopped short of the tree.

At the base of the tree was a hollow, its edges glowing with the same eerie light as the symbols etched into the bark. The whispers seemed to emanate from the hollow, drawing Lena and Ethan closer.

This is it, Ethan said, his voice barely audible. The heart.

Lena nodded, her chest tightening as she stared into the hollow. The mist surged around them, the shadows pressing closer, their crimson eyes burning like fire.

One must give, the voices chanted, their tone rising. *The bond must hold.*

Ethan stepped forward, his hand tightening around Lena's. Then take me, he said, his voice steady.

No! Lena cried, pulling him back. You can't—

I have to, he said, his dark eyes meeting hers. Lena, if this is the only way to save you, then it's worth it.

Tears streamed down her face as she clutched his arm. There has to be another way, she said, her voice breaking. We can find another way.

The whispers grew louder, the mist swirling violently around them. The shadows moved closer, their forms flickering and wavering as they encircled the tree.

And then, the ground trembled.

Twenty-Three

The Revelation

The ground beneath them quaked violently, sending tremors through the clearing as Lena and Ethan clung to each other. The ancient tree at the heart of the mist seemed to come alive, its roots twisting and curling, glowing faintly with the eerie light of the runes carved into its bark. The mist surged upward like a tidal wave, engulfing the clearing in an impenetrable haze. The whispers became deafening, overlapping into a chaotic, relentless chant.

One must give.

The bond must hold.

Lena tightened her grip on Ethan's arm, her voice trembling. We can't let it take us, she whispered, her tears falling freely. We can't.

Ethan's jaw clenched, his dark eyes locked on the glowing hollow at the base of the tree. If it comes to that, he said, his voice steady despite the chaos around them, it's me, Lena. Not you.

No! Lena shouted, her voice cracking. You don't get to make that choice.

Not alone.

Ethan turned to her, his expression hard but filled with an unspoken depth of emotion. I made it the moment I met you, he said quietly. You don't belong to this. You have a life—a future. I won't let the mist take that from you.

Lena shook her head fiercely, her hands trembling as she clutched the locket around her neck. Its warmth pulsed steadily, like a heartbeat, pushing back the icy grip of the mist. We can find another way, she said, desperation lacing her voice. There has to be another way.

Before Ethan could respond, the ground trembled again, and the mist parted. From the hollow at the base of the tree emerged a figure, its form faint and translucent, like a ghost suspended in time. Lena's breath caught as she recognized her.

Elise, she whispered.

The figure stepped forward, her movements slow and deliberate. She was just as Lena had seen her in the photographs—tall and graceful, her long dark hair framing her pale, ethereal face. But her eyes held a sorrow that seemed to pierce through Lena's chest.

Elise, Ethan said, his voice filled with disbelief. Is it really you?

The figure didn't answer immediately. Instead, she turned her gaze to Lena, her expression softening. You remind me so much of myself, Elise's voice was soft, almost melodic, but it carried an undercurrent of sorrow that resonated deep within Lena. You remind me so much of myself, she said again, her eyes lingering on Lena with a mix of warmth and regret. The same fire, the same determination to protect the ones you love.

Lena's throat tightened. Elise, she said, stepping forward cautiously. You...

you sacrificed yourself, didn't you? To save him?

Elise nodded slowly, her gaze drifting to Ethan. I did what I thought was right, she said. But the forest… the mist… it twists everything. It doesn't just take—it binds.

Ethan clenched his fists, his voice breaking. You didn't deserve this. None of this should have happened to you.

Elise's expression darkened, and the glow in her eyes dimmed. The mist doesn't care about deserving, she said. It cares about balance. About keeping the bond intact.

What bond? Lena demanded, her voice trembling. Why does it matter so much? Why does it have to take someone?

Elise turned back to Lena, her translucent form flickering slightly as the mist swirled around her. The bond is what keeps the forest alive, she explained. It's ancient, older than any of us. The mist feeds on the sacrifice, using it to sustain the balance between life and death.

Lena's stomach churned. And if the bond is broken?

Elise hesitated, her form flickering again. The forest would collapse, she said quietly. The mist would consume everything it touches, spreading beyond these trees. It would become unstoppable.

Ethan's jaw tightened. Then why not let it die? Why does the bond have to exist at all?

Elise's gaze softened, and she stepped closer to him. Because the forest is alive, she said. And like anything alive, it fights to survive. The mist isn't just a force—it's a will. It demands balance, and it will take what it needs to preserve it.

Lena clutched the locket around her neck, its warmth pulsing steadily against her skin. But there has to be another way, she said, her voice breaking. You said the bond can only be broken by a choice. What if we don't make it? What if we refuse?

Elise's expression grew somber. If you refuse, she said, the mist will choose for you. It will take what it wants, and you will have no say in the matter.

Lena's heart sank. She turned to Ethan, her tears blurring her vision. We can't let it take you, she said, her voice trembling. There has to be another way.

Ethan stepped forward, his hands gripping Lena's shoulders. Lena, he said firmly, if it comes to that, I won't let it take you. Do you hear me? I won't.

No! Lena shouted, her voice cracking. You don't get to decide that. We're in this together.

The mist swirled violently, the whispers growing louder and more frantic. Elise's form flickered and wavered, her translucent figure becoming harder to see. You must choose, she said, her voice fading. Before it's too late.

The ground trembled again, and the shadows that had been circling the clearing surged forward, their crimson eyes burning with an unnatural light. Lena and Ethan stepped back instinctively, their hands tightening around each other's.

The mist's voice rose above the whispers, its tone commanding and chilling. *One must give. The bond must hold.*

Ethan turned to Lena, his expression hardening. Lena, listen to me, he said urgently. If it comes down to it—

No! she interrupted, her voice filled with defiance. We'll find another way. I won't let you do this.

The mist surged closer, its tendrils curling around their ankles like chains. Lena's chest tightened as the oppressive weight pressed against her mind, making it hard to think. She clutched the locket tightly, its warmth pushing back the worst of the cold.

Elise! she shouted, her voice trembling. There has to be another way. Please, tell us what to do!

Elise's flickering form reappeared, her voice faint and strained. The heart of the mist is its anchor, she said. If you can destroy it, the bond will break.

Ethan frowned. And what happens then?

Elise hesitated, her translucent form wavering. The forest will die, she said quietly. And so will I.

Lena's breath caught in her throat. Elise, no—

I've been bound to this place for too long, Elise said, her voice soft but resolute. If breaking the bond means freeing you, then it's worth it.

The mist roared, its tendrils surging upward like a tidal wave. The shadows closed in, their forms flickering and shifting as they surrounded the clearing.

Go, Elise said, her voice breaking. Destroy the heart. End this.

Lena and Ethan exchanged a brief glance, their hands tightening around each other's. Then, without another word, they turned and ran toward the ancient tree, its glowing hollow pulsing like a heartbeat.

The mist howled in rage, its shadows chasing after them as the ground trembled beneath their feet. The whispers rose to a deafening crescendo, their chaotic symphony filling the air.

And somewhere behind them, Elise's voice echoed faintly: *Set me free.*

Twenty-Four

The Choice

The ancient tree loomed before them, its gnarled roots twisting into the earth like claws. The glowing hollow at its base pulsed with an otherworldly light, casting eerie shadows across the mist-shrouded clearing. The air was thick and heavy, filled with the sound of whispers that grew louder and more frenzied with every step Lena and Ethan took.

The bond must hold.

One must give.

The mist swirled violently, its tendrils rising and snapping like serpents, as though trying to drive them back. Shadows circled the clearing, their crimson eyes glowing like embers. The ground trembled beneath their feet, and the ancient tree groaned as though alive.

We're out of time, Ethan said, his voice strained as he tightened his grip on Lena's hand. It's now or never.

Lena's heart pounded in her chest as she stared at the hollow, its glow both mesmerizing and terrifying. She clutched the locket around her neck, its warmth pulsing steadily like a heartbeat. The weight of Elise's words pressed against her mind: *The heart of the mist is its anchor. Destroy it, and the bond will break.*

But if we destroy it, Lena whispered, her voice trembling, the forest will die. And so will Elise.

Ethan's jaw tightened, his gaze fixed on the tree. She wants this, he said. She asked us to set her free.

Lena shook her head, tears streaming down her face. There has to be another way, she said, her voice breaking. We can't just destroy everything. There has to be another way!

The mist roared in response, its tendrils surging toward them. Ethan pulled Lena behind him, his flashlight beam cutting through the haze. The shadows recoiled, their forms flickering and wavering, but they didn't retreat.

We don't have time to argue, Ethan said, his voice firm but laced with urgency. If we don't act now, the mist will take us both.

Lena's chest tightened as the whispers grew louder, pressing against her mind like a vice. She could feel the mist's presence all around her, suffocating and relentless, its voice echoing in her thoughts.

Choose.

Give.

The bond must hold.

Ethan turned to her, his dark eyes filled with determination. Lena, he said, his voice softening, you need to go. Let me finish this.

No, Lena said sharply, grabbing his arm. I'm not leaving you. We do this together.

Ethan's expression hardened, but before he could respond, the mist surged forward, its tendrils wrapping around his legs like chains. He stumbled, his hands grasping at the air as the mist began to pull him toward the tree.

Ethan! Lena screamed, grabbing his arm and pulling with all her strength. The mist's cold tendrils burned against her skin, but she refused to let go. I won't let it take you!

The locket around her neck glowed brighter, its warmth spreading through her body like fire. The mist recoiled slightly, its tendrils loosening their grip on Ethan. He gasped for air, his hands clutching hers as he struggled to stand.

Lena, he said, his voice trembling. The locket—it's protecting you.

She looked down at the pendant, its golden surface shining with a light that seemed to push back the darkness. A memory of Elise's voice echoed in her mind: *It's a piece of the bond, a fragment of what was taken. It's your connection to the mist—and to me.*

Lena's eyes widened as understanding dawned. The locket, she whispered. It's the key.

Ethan frowned, his breathing ragged. What do you mean?

Lena turned to him, her tears glistening in the dim light. If the locket is part of the bond, then maybe… maybe I can use it to sever the connection. To break the bond without destroying the forest.

Ethan's expression darkened. And what happens to you if you do that?

Lena hesitated, her hands trembling. I don't know, she admitted. But if it means saving you, it's worth it.

No, Ethan said firmly, his grip on her arm tightening. I'm not letting you risk yourself for me.

You don't get to decide that, Lena said, her voice rising. This isn't just about you. It's about all of us—Elise, the forest, everything. If this is the only way to end this without destroying everything, then I have to try.

The mist surged again, its tendrils snapping and writhing as the whispers reached a deafening crescendo. The shadows closed in, their movements erratic and frantic, as though sensing the bond's imminent collapse.

Lena, Ethan said urgently, his voice breaking. Don't do this. Please.

She turned to him, her tears falling freely as she cupped his face in her hands. I love you, she said softly, her voice trembling. And that's why I have to do this.

Before Ethan could stop her, Lena stepped toward the tree, the locket glowing brighter with each step. The mist roared, its tendrils lashing out, but the locket's light pushed them back, creating a path to the hollow.

Lena! Ethan shouted, his voice filled with desperation.

She turned back to him one last time, her heart breaking at the sight of his anguished expression. Trust me, she said, her voice steady despite the fear coursing through her. This is the only way.

With that, she reached the hollow and held the locket above it. The whispers grew louder, their voices rising in a chaotic symphony that filled the air. The locket's light flared, and the ground trembled beneath her feet.

The tree groaned, its roots twisting and writhing as the mist surged upward in a final, desperate wave. The shadows dissolved into the haze, their crimson eyes fading into darkness.

And then, there was silence.

Twenty-Five

The Final Clue

The forest fell eerily silent, the oppressive whispers fading into a void that felt both haunting and hollow. The mist retreated slightly, curling along the edges of the clearing like a wounded beast. Lena stood motionless at the base of the ancient tree, the locket in her hand glowing faintly as its warmth ebbed. Her chest heaved, and tears streamed down her face, but she refused to let herself falter.

Behind her, Ethan scrambled to his feet, his voice breaking the silence. Lena! he shouted, rushing toward her. What did you do?

She turned slowly, her legs trembling under the weight of her actions. I don't know, she admitted, her voice barely above a whisper. But it's not over.

The ground beneath them trembled again, and the tree groaned, its gnarled roots curling inward as though pulling away from the earth. The runes etched into its bark flickered, their glow fading in and out like a dying ember. The hollow at its base pulsed one final time before collapsing into darkness.

Ethan reached her side, his hands gripping her shoulders. Are you okay? he asked, his voice laced with fear and desperation.

I think so, she said, though her legs felt like jelly and her head spun. She clutched the locket tightly, its glow now reduced to a faint shimmer. The locket… it did something. It pushed the mist back, but—

A low rumble interrupted her, and both of them turned to face the tree. The mist surged forward again, denser than before, but it didn't lash out. Instead, it seemed to swirl with purpose, coiling around the base of the tree like a serpent guarding its prey.

It's still here, Ethan said grimly. We didn't destroy it.

No, Lena agreed, her voice trembling. We disrupted it, but the bond is still holding.

As if in response to her words, the mist parted slightly, revealing something new at the base of the tree. A small compartment, hidden until now, had appeared in the hollow, its edges glowing faintly with the same eerie light as the runes.

What is that? Lena asked, her heart pounding.

I don't know, Ethan said, stepping closer cautiously. But I think we're supposed to find out.

The mist seemed to shift as they approached, pulling back just enough to allow them access to the hidden compartment. Lena knelt beside it, her hands trembling as she reached out to touch its edges. The surface was smooth and warm, and the faint glow pulsed rhythmically, almost like a heartbeat.

It's safe, she said softly, though she wasn't sure how she knew.

Ethan crouched beside her, his flashlight illuminating the interior of the compartment. Inside lay a small object wrapped in what looked like ancient fabric. Lena reached for it carefully, her fingers brushing against the delicate wrapping. The fabric crumbled to dust as she lifted the object, revealing a locket nearly identical to the one around her neck.

It's another locket, Ethan said, his voice filled with wonder. But why?

Lena turned the locket over in her hands, her fingers tracing the intricate carvings etched into its surface. Unlike hers, this one bore a faint inscription along the edge. She squinted, struggling to make out the words in the dim light.

It says, 'To bind is to love,' she read aloud, her voice trembling. And below that… 'To unbind is to free.'

Ethan frowned. It's another piece of the bond, he said. But what does it mean?

Lena's mind raced as she clutched the locket tightly. Elise's words echoed in her mind: *The bond can only be broken by a choice. A sacrifice.*

She looked up at Ethan, her eyes wide. I think this locket belonged to Elise, she said. It's part of her story—part of what happened to her.

Ethan's jaw tightened. Then it's a clue, he said. The final piece of the puzzle.

The ground trembled again, and the mist surged forward, curling around their feet like icy chains. The whispers returned, louder and more insistent this time, their chaotic rhythm filling the air.

Choose.

Give.

The bond must hold.

Lena clutched the locket to her chest, her heart racing. I think… I think the bond is tied to both lockets, she said. Mine and this one. They're like anchors, keeping the mist connected to the forest.

Ethan's brow furrowed. If that's true, then what happens if we bring them together? If we… unbind them?

Lena hesitated, fear clawing at her chest. I don't know, she admitted. But it might be the only way to break the bond without destroying everything.

The mist howled, its tendrils rising like a tidal wave as the whispers reached a deafening crescendo. The clearing trembled, the tree groaning as its roots twisted violently.

We don't have much time, Ethan said urgently. Whatever we're going to do, we have to do it now.

Lena nodded, her hands trembling as she held both lockets. The warmth of her own locket surged, spreading through her like fire, while the second locket grew cold in her hands. The conflicting energies sent a shockwave through her body, making her gasp.

Are you okay? Ethan asked, his voice filled with concern.

Yes, she said, though her voice wavered. But this… this is going to be dangerous.

Ethan grabbed her hand, his grip steady and reassuring. We'll do it together, he said firmly. No matter what.

Lena took a deep breath, her tears falling freely as she looked at him. Together, she echoed.

As she brought the two lockets closer, the mist roared, its tendrils surging toward them with renewed fury. The light from her locket flared, pushing back the darkness, while the coldness of Elise's locket spread outward like frost.

The air around them crackled with energy, and the ground shook violently. The whispers blended into a single, deafening voice:

The bond must hold!

And then, the light exploded.

Twenty-Six

The Heart of the Mist

The explosion of light was blinding, enveloping the clearing in a brilliance so intense it seemed to burn away the mist itself. Lena felt the energy surge through her, a wave of fire and frost colliding within her chest. She clutched the two lockets tightly, their opposing forces pulling at her like magnets trying to tear her apart.

Ethan's voice cut through the chaos. Lena! he shouted, his hands gripping her shoulders as he tried to steady her. Let go!

I can't! she screamed, her voice trembling with pain. It's pulling me in!

The ground beneath them trembled violently, the ancient tree at the center of the clearing groaning as its roots twisted and writhed. The mist surged forward, its tendrils snapping and curling like angry serpents, but the light from the lockets pushed it back, creating a fragile bubble of safety around them.

The bond must hold, the mist roared, its voice a cacophony of rage and despair. *You cannot break it!*

Lena gasped, her knees buckling under the strain. She felt as though she were being torn apart, her body caught between the warmth of her own locket and the icy chill of Elise's. Images flashed through her mind—Elise standing at the edge of the forest, her face serene but haunted; Ethan's great-uncle reaching for her, his expression filled with love and despair; and the mist, swirling like a living thing, binding them together in an eternal, unbreakable bond.

It's too strong! Lena cried, her tears blurring her vision. I don't know if I can do this!

Yes, you can, Ethan said firmly, his hands gripping hers over the lockets. You're stronger than this. We're stronger than this. Together, remember?

His words cut through the chaos, grounding her. She met his gaze, her chest tightening at the raw determination in his eyes. Together, she echoed, her voice trembling but resolute.

She took a deep breath, her grip on the lockets tightening. The warmth of her locket surged again, pushing back the icy chill of Elise's, and for a moment, the two energies seemed to merge, creating a pulse of pure, radiant light.

The mist howled in response, its tendrils lashing out desperately. The shadows that had been circling the clearing surged forward, their crimson eyes blazing with fury. The whispers rose to a deafening crescendo, a single, desperate command:

The bond must hold!

Lena's heart pounded as the energy in the lockets reached a fever pitch. The warmth and coldness collided, sending shockwaves through her body. She felt as though she were standing on the edge of a precipice, the weight of the forest's fate pressing down on her.

Elise! she shouted, her voice breaking. Help me! Please!

The light from the lockets flared again, and suddenly, Elise appeared. Her translucent form flickered like a dying flame, but her expression was calm, resolute.

You're almost there, Elise said, her voice soft but steady. You have to let go, Lena. Let the bond break.

Lena's chest tightened. But what if it destroys everything? What if—

It won't, Elise said, stepping closer. The bond is tied to me. When it breaks, the mist will lose its hold, and the forest will be free. But you have to trust yourself. Trust me.

Lena's tears fell freely as she nodded, her hands trembling as she held the lockets. I'm scared, she admitted, her voice barely above a whisper.

I know, Elise said gently. But you're stronger than your fear.

Ethan squeezed her hands, his voice steady. We've got this, Lena. Together.

She took a deep breath, her resolve hardening. With one final surge of strength, she brought the lockets together, their opposing energies colliding in a blinding flash of light. The clearing erupted with energy, the ground shaking violently as the ancient tree groaned and split down the middle.

The mist let out a final, ear-piercing roar, its tendrils thrashing wildly before dissolving into the light. The shadows faded, their crimson eyes flickering and dying like embers in a dying fire. The whispers stopped, replaced by a profound, almost deafening silence.

Lena collapsed to her knees, the lockets falling from her hands as the light slowly faded. She gasped for air, her body trembling from the effort. Ethan was beside her in an instant, his arms wrapping around her protectively.

Lena, he said urgently, his voice filled with concern. Are you okay? Talk to me.

She nodded weakly, leaning into him for support. I think… I think it's over.

The ancient tree stood silent and still, its roots no longer twisting or writhing. The glowing runes on its bark had dimmed, and the hollow at its base was empty, the light within extinguished. The forest around them was quiet, the mist gone, leaving only the faint sound of the wind rustling through the trees.

Elise's translucent form appeared one last time, her expression serene. She stepped toward Lena and Ethan, her gaze filled with gratitude.

You did it, Elise said softly. The bond is broken. The forest is free.

Lena's throat tightened as she looked at Elise. And you? she asked, her voice trembling. What happens to you?

Elise smiled faintly, her form flickering. I'll be free too, she said. It's time for me to rest.

Tears streamed down Lena's face as she reached out, her hand passing through Elise's fading form. Thank you, she whispered. For everything.

Elise nodded, her expression filled with peace. Thank you, she said, her voice growing faint. For finishing what I couldn't.

With that, her form dissolved into light, scattering into the wind like golden fireflies. The forest seemed to sigh, the weight of the mist's presence finally lifting.

Lena leaned against Ethan, her chest heaving as the enormity of what they had done sank in. It's over, she said softly, her voice filled with relief and exhaustion.

Ethan held her tightly, his own tears glistening in the fading light. It's over, he echoed.

But as they sat together in the silent clearing, a faint, lingering glow caught Lena's eye. The lockets, lying side by side in the grass, still shimmered faintly, their light pulsing like a heartbeat.

Twenty-Seven

The Sacrifice

The air in the clearing was eerily still. The mist was gone, but the oppressive silence that remained felt like a void, stretching endlessly around Lena and Ethan. The lockets lay in the grass, their faint, rhythmic glow the only indication that the bond's story wasn't entirely over.

Lena's fingers trembled as she reached for the lockets. The warmth of hers had faded, replaced by a coldness that sent a shiver through her. Ethan knelt beside her, his dark eyes fixed on the glowing objects. He placed a steadying hand on her shoulder.

Careful, he said, his voice low.

Lena hesitated, her chest tightening as the locket's faint glow pulsed under her fingertips. It feels… different, she murmured. Like it's waiting for something.

Ethan frowned, his brow furrowing. Waiting for what?

Before Lena could respond, the ground beneath them trembled again. It was a faint vibration, but it sent a jolt of panic through her. The ancient tree groaned, its cracked trunk shifting slightly, as though the forest itself was stirring.

Lena turned to Ethan, her breath quickening. I thought it was over, she said, her voice trembling. We broke the bond.

We did, Ethan said firmly, though his expression betrayed his uncertainty. But maybe… He trailed off, his gaze falling to the lockets. Maybe there's something else.

The glow of the lockets intensified, their pulsing light growing stronger. Lena pulled her hand back instinctively, the coldness of the metal biting into her skin. The whispers, which had vanished with the mist, returned faintly, threading through the silence like ghostly tendrils.

One must give.

The bond must hold.

Lena's stomach churned. No, she whispered, shaking her head. We broke it. We ended this.

Ethan's jaw tightened. The mist is gone, he said. But maybe the bond isn't just about the mist. Maybe it's something deeper—something tied to us.

Lena's chest tightened, the weight of his words pressing against her. You mean… the bond isn't just broken? It needs to be replaced?

Ethan didn't answer immediately. He knelt beside the lockets, his expression hardening as he studied their glowing forms. It's possible, he said finally. Elise said the bond was tied to her. If we broke that connection, then maybe the forest needs something—or someone—else to take her place.

Lena's heart sank. No, she said sharply. There has to be another way. We can't just—

The whispers grew louder, cutting her off. The light from the lockets flared, and the clearing was bathed in an ethereal glow. The ancient tree groaned again, its roots twisting and curling into the earth.

The forest was demanding its price.

Ethan stood abruptly, his fists clenching at his sides. If it's someone the forest needs, he said, his voice steady, then it's going to be me.

No! Lena cried, grabbing his arm. You can't do this, Ethan. I won't let you.

Ethan turned to her, his dark eyes filled with determination. Lena, listen to me, he said firmly. This is the only way. The forest needs a sacrifice to survive. If it doesn't get one, everything Elise did—everything we did—will have been for nothing.

Tears streamed down Lena's face as she shook her head. There has to be another way, she said, her voice breaking. We can't just let it take you.

Ethan cupped her face in his hands, his touch gentle despite the tension in his body. Lena, he said softly, this isn't just about me. It's about you. About giving you a chance to live, to be free.

I don't want to be free without you, Lena whispered, her tears falling onto his hands. I can't lose you.

Ethan's lips pressed into a thin line, his own tears glistening in the glow of the lockets. You won't lose me, he said. Not really. I'll always be with you.

The light from the lockets flared again, brighter and more intense. The whispers grew louder, overlapping into a single, insistent command:

Choose.

Ethan stepped toward the lockets, but Lena grabbed his arm, her grip fierce. No, she said, her voice trembling but resolute. If anyone's going to do this, it's me.

Ethan froze, his dark eyes wide with shock. Lena, no—

It has to be me, she said, cutting him off. I'm the one who connected with Elise. I'm the one who broke the bond. If the forest needs someone, it's me.

Ethan shook his head, his voice rising. No! I'm not letting you do this, Lena. I won't let you.

You don't get to decide that, she said fiercely, her tears streaming down her face. This is my choice.

The ground trembled violently, the light from the lockets pulsing like a heartbeat. The whispers rose to a deafening crescendo, their command echoing through the clearing:

Choose.

Lena turned to Ethan, her chest tightening as she saw the anguish in his eyes. I love you, she said softly, her voice breaking. And that's why I have to do this.

No, Ethan said, his voice cracking. Lena, please—

But before he could stop her, Lena stepped toward the lockets, the light enveloping her like a cocoon. The coldness of Elise's locket spread through her, colliding with the warmth of her own, and for a moment, everything was silent.

The whispers stopped. The ground stilled. The forest held its breath.

And then, the light exploded.

Twenty-Eight

Breaking the Curse

The explosion of light consumed the clearing, obliterating the mist and shadows in an instant. The ancient tree at the heart of the clearing groaned loudly, its massive trunk splitting apart, revealing a core of pulsating energy. The runes on its bark flared one last time before dimming entirely, leaving the forest shrouded in silence.

Ethan was thrown back by the force of the blast, landing hard on the ground. The searing light burned in his vision as he scrambled to his feet, shouting Lena's name. Lena! he cried, his voice raw and desperate.

But she was gone.

The clearing was empty, save for the faint glow of the two lockets lying at the base of the shattered tree. Ethan's heart twisted painfully as he stumbled forward, his legs trembling beneath him. The air was heavy, oppressive, and yet eerily calm. The whispers had vanished, replaced by an unnatural stillness.

He dropped to his knees before the lockets, his hands shaking as he reached for them. They were cold now, their glow fading like embers in a dying fire. Lena, he whispered, clutching the lockets tightly. No. No, no, no…

Tears blurred his vision as he pressed the lockets to his chest, his breath hitching. You can't be gone, he said, his voice cracking. You promised we'd do this together. You promised…

The clearing seemed to echo his grief, the silence pressing against him like a physical weight. The tree's shattered trunk stood as a grim reminder of what they had sacrificed. Ethan's chest tightened, and a deep, aching emptiness settled over him.

And then, a faint warmth spread through his hands.

He froze, his tears falling onto the lockets as their light flickered faintly. The warmth grew stronger, spreading through his body like fire, and a familiar voice echoed in his mind.

Ethan.

His head snapped up, his heart pounding. Lena? he whispered, his voice trembling.

The light from the lockets flared briefly, and a figure began to materialize in the center of the clearing. At first, it was faint and indistinct, like a wisp of smoke caught in the wind. But as the light grew stronger, the figure became clearer.

It was Lena.

Ethan's breath caught as she stepped forward, her form shimmering with an ethereal glow. Her face was pale but serene, her eyes filled with a mixture of sorrow and love. She looked at him, her lips curving into a faint smile.

Ethan, she said softly, her voice carrying the warmth that had always grounded him.

He surged to his feet, his legs nearly giving out as he stumbled toward her. Lena! he cried, his voice breaking. You're… you're here.

She nodded, her tears glistening in the dim light. I'm here, she said, her voice trembling. But not for long.

Ethan froze, his chest tightening. What do you mean? We broke the bond. The mist is gone. You're safe now.

Lena shook her head, her expression bittersweet. The bond was tied to Elise, she said. When we broke it, the forest needed a new anchor. I made the choice to take her place.

Ethan's heart sank, his hands trembling. No, he said fiercely. We were supposed to end this. Together. You weren't supposed to—

I had to, Lena said, stepping closer. It was the only way. The forest needed balance, and I couldn't let it take you.

Ethan's tears fell freely as he reached for her, his fingers brushing against her glowing form. She was warm and solid, yet he could feel the faint hum of energy beneath her skin—a reminder that she was no longer entirely human.

There has to be a way to bring you back, he said desperately. Tell me what to do. I'll do anything.

Lena shook her head, her eyes glistening. The bond is stronger than both of us, she said. I'm tied to the forest now. But it's different. The mist is gone. The forest is free. And so am I.

Ethan's breath hitched, his hands gripping her shoulders. Free? he asked, his voice breaking. You call this freedom? You're bound to this place. You can't leave.

Lena cupped his face in her hands, her touch gentle but firm. I chose this, she said softly. For you. For us. And I don't regret it.

The light around her began to fade, her form growing fainter. Ethan's chest tightened as he realized what was happening. No, he said, his voice trembling. Don't go. Please, Lena, don't leave me.

I'll always be with you, she said, her voice steady despite the tears streaming down her face. In the forest. In the wind. In every sunrise.

Ethan's hands clutched at her desperately, but she was already slipping away. Lena, he whispered, his voice breaking. I love you.

She smiled, her tears glistening in the fading light. I love you too, she said. Always.

And then, she was gone.

The clearing was silent once more, the warmth of her presence lingering like an echo. Ethan fell to his knees, the lockets still clutched tightly in his hands. His tears fell freely as he stared at the empty space where she had stood, his heart shattered.

But as the first rays of sunlight broke through the canopy above, he felt a faint breeze brush against his cheek, carrying the scent of wildflowers and earth. He closed his eyes, his chest tightening as the wind whispered her name.

Lena.

Twenty-Nine

The Aftermath

The sun climbed higher, casting golden light over the clearing where moments ago the heart of the mist had pulsed with an ominous life. Now, all was still. The air was crisp and clear, a sharp contrast to the oppressive fog that had consumed the forest for so long. The ancient tree stood fractured, its gnarled roots no longer twisting or pulsing. It was merely a tree now, a shell of what it once was.

Ethan sat on the forest floor, his back against the broken tree, clutching the two lockets in his trembling hands. His breath was ragged, and his chest ached with the weight of his grief. The forest around him was alive with the sounds of birdsong and rustling leaves, but they felt distant, hollow. The world seemed brighter, yet dimmer all at once.

Lena, he whispered, his voice cracking as he turned the lockets over in his hands. The one that had belonged to Elise was cold, its carvings faint and worn, while Lena's still held a faint warmth, as though a piece of her lingered within.

The lockets pulsed faintly, their rhythms matching the beat of his heart. Ethan frowned, holding them closer to his chest. The warmth spread through him, subtle and comforting, but it did little to fill the void she had left behind.

The walk back to the cabin was slow and arduous. Every step felt like a betrayal, as though moving forward meant leaving Lena behind. The forest around him was unrecognizable now. Where the mist had once choked the air, sunlight streamed through the canopy, illuminating patches of wildflowers and moss. The shadows no longer lingered threateningly; instead, they danced lightly in the breeze.

When he reached the cabin, Ethan hesitated at the threshold. The place felt emptier now, stripped of the tension and unease that had clung to it like a second skin. He pushed the door open and stepped inside, the floorboards creaking beneath his weight.

Her sketchbook was still on the table, open to a drawing of the ancient tree. The lines were bold and confident, capturing its eerie beauty with stunning accuracy. Ethan traced the edge of the page with his finger, his throat tightening.

You were always so much better at seeing the truth, he murmured, his voice barely audible.

He sat down heavily, placing the lockets on the table. They pulsed faintly, their light casting soft shadows on the worn wood. Ethan stared at them, his mind racing with unanswered questions. What had Lena truly given to the forest? Was she bound to it forever, or was there still a way to bring her back?

Days passed in a blur. Ethan stayed in the cabin, unable to bring himself to leave the forest. He wandered the trails they had walked together, his steps aimless and his thoughts heavy. The forest was peaceful now, its beauty unmarred by the mist, but it felt empty without her.

One evening, as the sun dipped below the horizon, Ethan found himself back in the clearing. The ancient tree stood silent and still, its hollow dark and empty. He knelt at its base, the lockets clutched tightly in his hands.

I don't know if you can hear me, he said softly, his voice trembling. But if you can... I need you to know that I'm not giving up. I'll find a way to bring you back. I don't care how long it takes.

The wind stirred around him, carrying the faint scent of wildflowers. Ethan closed his eyes, his chest tightening as the breeze brushed against his cheek. It was so faint, but he swore he could hear her voice—soft and distant, like a memory carried on the wind.

I'm still here.

The next morning, Ethan awoke to the sound of birdsong outside the cabin. He sat up slowly, his body aching from days of restless sleep. The lockets lay on the table beside him, their light stronger now, pulsing in rhythm with the sunlight streaming through the window.

He frowned, reaching for them. The warmth of Lena's locket was undeniable now, spreading through his fingers like a gentle fire. It felt alive, almost as if it were trying to communicate.

What are you trying to tell me? he whispered, holding the locket closer.

As if in response, the carvings on Lena's locket glowed faintly. The light spread to Elise's locket, their pulses synchronizing. The runes seemed to shift, rearranging themselves into a new pattern that Ethan hadn't seen before.

It wasn't just decorative. It was a map.

Ethan's breath caught as the realization hit him. The carvings weren't just designs—they were directions, pointing to a place deeper within the forest. A place he and Lena hadn't explored.

Is this…? he murmured, his voice trembling. Is this you?

The lockets glowed brighter, their light illuminating the map clearly. Ethan's heart raced as he studied the markings, his mind spinning with possibilities. Was this a way to bring Lena back? Or was it her way of guiding him to something she couldn't finish herself?

He stood abruptly, grabbing his flashlight and a bag of supplies. His chest tightened with a mix of hope and fear as he stepped out of the cabin and into the forest. The sunlight filtered through the trees, illuminating his path, but his focus was on the map etched into the lockets.

I'm coming, Lena, he said softly, his voice steady despite the storm of emotions raging inside him. Whatever this is, I'll find it. I'll find you.

The forest seemed to hum with energy as he walked, the path ahead growing darker and more mysterious. But Ethan didn't falter. The faint glow of the lockets guided him, their warmth a constant reminder that Lena was still with him—somehow.

And he wouldn't stop until he brought her back.

Thirty

Fading Into Mist

The forest grew darker as Ethan followed the path etched into the lockets. The markings had been faint at first, their meaning elusive, but as he ventured deeper into the woods, they seemed to pulse with clarity, lighting the way. The trees towered above him, their branches twisting together like a cathedral ceiling, shrouding the path in shadow. The forest was alive, but not in the way it had been under the mist's oppressive rule. It breathed with a quiet, serene energy, as though it had been waiting for this moment.

Ethan's steps quickened, his heart racing as the map led him toward a part of the forest he had never seen before. The air grew cooler, and the faint scent of wildflowers lingered, carried by a gentle breeze. He clutched the lockets tightly, their warmth steady against his palm. Whatever lay ahead, he knew Lena was guiding him.

Finally, the path opened into a small glade bathed in soft, golden light. At its center stood a pool of crystal-clear water, surrounded by wildflowers that swayed gently despite the absence of wind. The lockets pulsed faintly, their glow reflected in the water's surface.

Ethan approached cautiously, his breath hitching as he knelt beside the pool. The water shimmered, its surface rippling as though it were alive. He held the lockets over the pool, their light growing brighter with every passing moment.

What now? he murmured, his voice trembling.

As if in response, the carvings on the lockets shifted again, the runes rearranging themselves into a single word:

Believe.

Ethan's chest tightened, his tears blurring his vision. Lena, he whispered, his voice breaking. If you can hear me… if you're still here… I believe.

He placed the lockets gently in the water, their light merging into a single, radiant beam that pierced the surface. The pool glowed brighter, the energy spreading outward in rippling waves. The air around him hummed with power, and the wildflowers seemed to lean toward the pool, their petals glowing faintly.

And then, she appeared.

Lena rose from the water, her form shimmering with light. She was translucent at first, like a reflection in glass, but as the glow from the pool intensified, she became solid, real. Her dark hair cascaded over her shoulders, her eyes wide with wonder as she took in her surroundings.

Ethan, she said softly, her voice filled with disbelief.

He didn't hesitate. He surged forward, wrapping his arms around her as tears streamed down his face. Lena, he whispered, his voice trembling. You're here. You're really here.

She clung to him, her own tears falling freely. I didn't think… I didn't know if I'd ever see you again, she said, her voice breaking.

You saved me, Ethan said, pulling back just enough to look into her eyes. You saved all of us. I couldn't let it end like that. I couldn't let you go.

Lena smiled, her tears glistening in the golden light. You brought me back, she said. I don't know how, but you did.

The light from the pool began to fade, its glow retreating into the water until the glade was bathed in the soft, natural light of the setting sun. The lockets floated gently to the surface, their light extinguished but their warmth still palpable. Ethan reached for them, placing them in Lena's hands.

These belong to you now, he said, his voice steady. Both of them.

She looked down at the lockets, her fingers tracing the carvings. They're more than just objects, she said. They're symbols of everything we've been through. Everything we've fought for.

Ethan nodded, his hand brushing against hers. They're a part of us.

Lena met his gaze, her eyes filled with love. And so are you, she said softly.

They left the glade together, the path ahead illuminated by the soft glow of the setting sun. The forest around them was quiet, peaceful, as though it had been reborn. The mist was gone, its oppressive weight lifted, leaving behind a world that felt new and alive.

As they walked, Lena leaned into Ethan, her steps steady but cautious. Do you think it's really over? she asked, her voice tinged with uncertainty.

Ethan wrapped an arm around her, his touch reassuring. The mist is gone, he said. The bond is broken. But the forest is still here. It's different now, freer. And so are we.

Lena nodded, her fingers brushing against the lockets in her pocket. I feel it, she said. It's like the forest is healing.

Ethan smiled, his gaze fixed on the horizon. And so are we.

As they reached the edge of the forest, the first stars began to appear in the twilight sky. Lena turned back, her eyes lingering on the towering trees and the soft glow of the glade in the distance.

Do you think she's still here? she asked, her voice barely above a whisper.

Ethan followed her gaze, his expression thoughtful. Elise gave everything to save this place, he said. And you gave everything to save me. I think… I think she's at peace now. And maybe, in some way, she's still watching over us.

Lena smiled faintly, her tears glistening in the starlight. I hope so.

They stepped out of the forest together, the weight of their journey behind them but the promise of a new future ahead. The lockets pulsed faintly in Lena's pocket, their warmth a comforting reminder of the bond they had shared—and the love that had saved them.

As they walked hand in hand into the night, the forest behind them seemed to exhale, its shadows fading into mist.

Thirty-One

Epilogue

Far in the distance, beyond the glade, the faint silhouette of Elise and Ethan's great-uncle appeared, standing together beneath the ancient tree. Their faces were serene, their forms shimmering with light as they watched Lena and Ethan disappear into the horizon. The forest was quiet, the mist gone, but the memory of their love lingered—a reminder that even in the darkest of places, love had the power to heal, to save, and to endure.

And as the last traces of the mist faded into the starlit sky, the forest stood as a testament to the choices that had been made, the sacrifices that had been given, and the unbreakable bond that had brought them home.

The End.